The king-s..... hold them both.

Carlie saw no reason for either of them to spend an uncomfortable night.

She sat up and slipped her hand into his. "We'll both sleep in the bedroom."

Sean's eyes went wide. "But you don't remember me."

"I won't put you out of your bed."

"I'll be fine on the couch."

Carlie refused to believe he wanted her to leave him alone. Although Sean seemed to be a lone wolf, fit and capable of taking care of himself, she wanted to help him ease his grief.

"Even if I can't remember our wedding vows, we are husband and wife."

Sean took her by the shoulders, shaking her. "Let me get this straight. You want to share my bed tonight...."

Dear Intrigue Reader,

A brand-new year, the launch of a new millennium, a new cover look—and another exciting lineup of pulse-pounding romance and exhilarating suspense from Harlequin Intrigue!

This month, Amanda Stevens gives new meaning to the phrase "men in uniform" with her new trilogy, GALLAGHER JUSTICE, about a family of Chicago cops. They're tough, tender and totally to die for. Detective John Gallagher draws first blood in *The Littlest Witness* (#549).

If you've never been *Captured by a Sheikh* (#550), you don't know what you're missing! Veteran romance novelist Jacqueline Diamond takes you on a magic carpet ride you'll never forget, when a sheikh comes to claim his son, a baby he's never even seen.

Wouldn't you just love to wake up and have the sexiest man you've ever seen take you and your unborn child into his protection? Well, Harlequin Intrigue author Dani Sinclair does just that when she revisits FOOLS POINT. *My Baby, My Love* (#551) is the second story set in the Maryland town Dani created in her Harlequin Intrigue book *For His Daughter* (#539).

Susan Kearney rounds out the month with a trip to the wildest American frontier—Alaska. *A Night Without End* (#552) is another installment in the Harlequin Intrigue bestselling amnesia promotion A MEMORY AWAY.... This time a woman wakes to find herself in a remote land in the arms of a sexy stranger who claims to be her husband.

And this is just the beginning! We at Harlequin Intrigue are committed to keeping you on the edge of your seat. Thank you for your enthusiastic support.

Sincerely,

Denise O'Sullivan
Associate Senior Editor, Harlequin Intrigue

A Night Without End
Susan Kearney

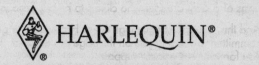

HARLEQUIN®

TORONTO • NEW YORK • LONDON
AMSTERDAM • PARIS • SYDNEY • HAMBURG
STOCKHOLM • ATHENS • TOKYO • MILAN • MADRID
PRAGUE • WARSAW • BUDAPEST • AUCKLAND

ISBN 0-373-22552-0

A NIGHT WITHOUT END

Visit us at www.romance.net

Printed in U.S.A.

ABOUT THE AUTHOR

Susan Kearney likes suspense-packed romance with an unforgettable twist. She's also more than fond of feisty heroines and heroes with soft hearts and hard heads. Sue lives in Florida with her husband, two children and two Boston terriers.

Books by Susan Kearney

HARLEQUIN INTRIGUE

Don't miss any of our special offers. Write to us at the following address for information on our newest releases.

Harlequin Reader Service
U.S.: 3010 Walden Ave., P.O. Box 1325, Buffalo, NY 14269
Canadian: P.O. Box 609, Fort Erie, Ont. L2A 5X3

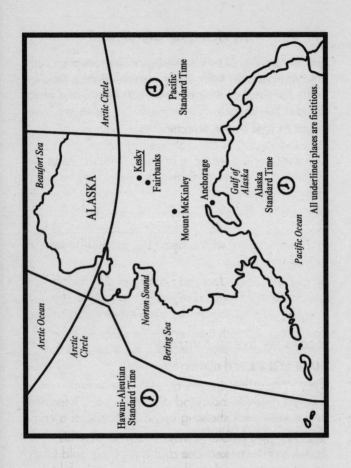

All underlined places are fictitious.

CAST OF CHARACTERS

Carlie Myers—A policewoman whose murky memory couldn't call up the previous two years. She's determined to discover her past so she can have a future.

Sean McCabe—An educated man who is just as experienced in a rough mining camp, a sophisticated boardroom or the bedroom. Sean claims he's Carlie's husband. So why does he seem like a stranger?

Jackson McCabe—The murder victim and Sean McCabe's adopted father. Jackson was a back woodsman with a heart big enough to take in a homeless boy.

Roger McCabe—Jackson's angry and grieving brother. But is Roger really grieving or does he have something to gain by his brother's death?

Ian Finley—A rich banker with a stake in Sean's mine. He's prosperous and has his finger on the pulse of the small mining town.

Tyler—Were his dreams of gold a delusion? Caught between boyhood and manhood, Tyler has a propensity for showing up at the scene of a crime.

Marvin—A gambler always ready to play his hand. With a poker face and a flashing gold tooth, Marvin stands back and watches events unfold— with seemingly no reason to commit murder.

Sally—Jackson's lady friend who is ready to move on. Did she really love Jackson or was it his money she wanted?

For Angela Catalano, my editor,
whose invaluable help is very much appreciated.

And for B.C., who gives excellent advice. Thank you.

Prologue

"Did I hear right? Did you say Alaska?" Carlie Myer propped one hip against the kitchen counter, twisted the phone cord and tried to keep the trembling from her voice.

Her husband, Bill, preoccupied and even more secretive than usual, hadn't been himself lately, but now his former bubbling enthusiasm returned to his voice and came in loud and clear from his car's cell phone. "I want to show you Chikosh Pass in summertime."

Perhaps she'd let him talk her into going on an Alaskan vacation, after all. Besides, relief from the tropical heat of August in Tampa, Florida might not be so bad.

If she didn't know better, from the way he described Alaska, she'd have thought he longed for his old job back. He was practically crooning into the telephone with his husky bedroom voice that he knew she had difficulty refusing. "You haven't lived until you've kayaked blue glacial rivers and climbed Mount Kiska—"

"You know I don't like the cold." Or the wilderness. She was a city girl, born and bred in the Sunshine State. And nothing relaxed her better than Florida sun, palm trees swishing in a seventy-five-degree breeze and the aroma of suntan oil on a white-sand beach.

"Come on, Carlie. It'll be romantic. The aurora borealis is unbelievable at night."

"So are the mosquitoes that suck a human being dry in half an hour—"

"Think of camping with the scent of spruce in your hair. Fresh salmon baked the way you like it—"

"What about grizzlies?"

Even if she accompanied him to Fairbanks, his intention to revisit his old haunts raised issues she preferred to forget. He made the trip sound so sentimental and appealing, but he had almost died in those frigid mountains he loved.

"You can sleep with your gun under the pillow," Bill teased.

In spite of her suspicions, Carlie allowed a smile to surface. A seven-year veteran of the Tampa Police Department, she considered her sidearm as necessary as most women did a tube of lipstick. However, on their wedding night, Bill had insisted he wasn't sharing her with a .357 Magnum and urged her to leave the weapon on her nightstand—a small compromise she'd made after the happiness he'd given her. That she was considering a trip to practically the North Pole was a testament to how much she loved him.

Every so often she had to remind herself that even the best marriage required compromises. If he wanted to return to Alaska, she'd go along with his request, but not before making one of her own.

"This is strictly a *vacation,* right?"

"And what else would it be? I'm a happily married man."

The thought of running into one of his old girlfriends was the least of her worries. And he knew it.

"No digging into unsolved cases?" she asked. Bill had worked for Customs in Alaska before he'd received a promotion and transferred to Florida. And he was damned secretive about his work. For all she knew he was still on the same case that had almost taken his life. Fear curdled in her gut. "Promise me, you've put the past behind you."

"Now, honey, we're just taking a little visit, and I may check out a few things. You aren't going to lose me. There's nothing to fear—"

Through the receiver, car horns blared in her ear. Metal screeched. Glass shattered.

"Bill? Bill! Talk to me, damn it."

His car phone went dead.

"God, no. Please, please, please don't do this to me."

With frantic fingers, she redialed his number, but the call wouldn't go through. Pain and panic slammed into her. Numbly, she tried the police department next.

But she didn't need anyone to tell her he was dead. Every cell in her body shuddered as the special connection they had shared was brutally severed.

He was gone. She would never again see his warm smile, never again hear his husky laughter or feel the comfort of his embrace. She wrapped her arms around herself to stop the shaking, but the gesture did nothing to halt the tears raging down her cheeks or the shivers crawling over her soul.

Bill was gone.

And deep in her heart she knew the fear had just begun.

Chapter One

Fifteen months later

The herd of elk spooked, taking off on a mad run, and, on the alert, Sean McCabe instantly froze. He read danger in the Alaskan bush easily, rapidly and expertly. While many Alaskans were at home in the woods, his senses were more acute than most, and years in these mountains had endowed him with almost a sixth sense. His ears picked up not just normal animal activity—but the lack of noise. An arctic warbler in the willow thicket had ceased to sing.

Sean did not move, all senses keenly focused. The abnormal stillness spoke to him. In the bush, game could be frightened by an angered grizzly, an approaching storm, a forest fire or an imminent earthquake. But he didn't see any bear signs, didn't smell smoke, and though he expected snow within hours, the sky remained blue and clear. Still, his neck prickled with an acute perception of danger and he shifted his stance with vigilant caution.

Well aware wildlife could sense vibrations in the ground long before people felt an earthquake, Sean dumped his heavy backpack of supplies and sprinted toward the Dog Mush Mine. If a tremor were to hit, he might have only moments to warn Jackson, who was most likely prospecting deep in the cave and unaware of the unusual stillness on the mountain.

A Sitka black-tailed deer bolted past Sean into a stand of white spruce and disappeared behind a hummock. A woodchuck dived for its burrow while a snowshoe hare bounded through the gooseberry bushes. Forcing his feet faster along the steep, well-trod trail, he redoubled his effort to reach his partner. And friend.

Jackson was family, the father he'd never had. Twenty years ago when Sean had been a lost and lonely eight-year-old brat, he'd run away from the very thought of a foster home, and the old prospector had taken him in. At first he'd been afraid of the miner, but he soon learned Jackson's gruff exterior hid a heart of melted gold nuggets. He'd taken in a hungry and defiant boy, fed him and educated him, given him the tools to make a living.

An eagle wheeled in the sky with a cacophony of cries. With a primal caution, Sean rounded the last bend in the trail, his boots pounding the hard-packed dirt. A bone-chilling gust pummeled him, but as he dashed into the mine past Jackson's bivouac site, the sheer rock pinnacle cut the wind. An eerie stillness made the hairs on the back of Sean's hands stand on end.

"Jackson! Get out! You hear me, there's an—"

Sean skidded to a halt. In the dim light of the mine, two bodies lay in the dirt. He had no trouble spotting Jackson's yellow Arctic parka.

"Jackson? You okay?"

Heart jackhammering, Sean reached out and touched the old prospector's neck, searching for a pulse. His body still warm, Jackson didn't let out so much as a moan. Sean couldn't find any reassuring evidence of a heartbeat.

No!

He leaned over Jackson, desperate for a sign that he still lived, straining for the slightest whisper of a breath.

He didn't move. He didn't breathe.

Gently Sean turned the man over. Blood drenched the yellow jacket, soaked into the dirt. And now he knew what had spooked the game.

Death.

No! Not Jackson. Not the man who meant the world to him. It couldn't be true.

A gaping wound and fresh blood on Jackson's chest indicated that the old prospector had been stabbed just minutes ago. Sean's vision clouded with a red rage. Spinning on his heel, he slammed his fist into the wall, welcoming the pain in his knuckles, wishing it took his mind off the agony of his loss.

Sean barely glanced at the second body. That Jackson had killed his attacker didn't satisfy him.

Jackson was the only father Sean had ever known. Unrelated by blood yet bonded by their love of this wild land, the willful boy and the crotchety old prospector had made a family. And now he was gone.

Murdered.

Murdered in the mine he loved.

Jackson's open eyes were frozen in surprise, horror and pain. The look of a man betrayed.

Sean ached to take out his grief and frustration with his fists. Instead, he ruthlessly quashed his anger, sank onto the floor and cradled his adoptive father's head on his lap. Rocking, Sean smoothed back Jackson's hair, gently closed his eyes.

He couldn't be dead.

But Sean couldn't deny the truth of the cooling body in his arms.

"I'm sorry, old man. I should have been here sooner. I should have been here when you needed me most." His eyes filled with tears. He could say no more. Just sat in the cold, rocking Jackson, feeling his warmth slip away and his body grow cold.

Finally, Sean stood on legs grown numb and floated a blanket over the body. Authorities needed to be notified. He pushed his choking grief deep inside and reached for the walkie-talkie clipped onto his belt.

He pressed the talk button, cleared his throat to make the words come out. "Sean to base."

"Marvin here," answered the radio operator.

"I'm at the Dog Mush. Jackson's dead."

"Come again. Did you say dead?"

"Murdered." The word tasted bitter in Sean's mouth.

"I'm sorry. Real sorry. I liked that old man."

Jackson and Marvin had played poker every Friday night for years. Was Sean imagining the voice choked with tears coming over the radio or did they have poor reception?

"Any sign of who killed him?"

"Looks like Jackson took out the other guy before

he died. Send up a couple of men with sleds for the bodies.''

''Roger that. Anything else?''

''Notify the authorities in Fairbanks.''

''Will do. Base out.''

Sean's attention turned from Jackson to the smaller man who lay unmoving on his back in the dirt, the bloody knife still in his hand. Who was he? He faced away from Sean and a hood partially covered his face, and Sean didn't recognize the pea-green jacket or the barely broken-in boots. Perhaps his pockets held identification.

Sean knelt beside the murderer, wishing he was still alive—so he could slam a fist into his face, close his hands around his throat and kill him again. If his thoughts were vicious and primitive, at least they were honest. He'd spent eight years in the civilized east, learning that an Italian suit and tie could hide men as vicious and deadly as grizzlies. He preferred the uncrowded mountains, the unpolluted air and the sweat equity of his rough-hewn log cabin to the greedy and callous life in the big cities.

He liked to think of these mountains as pristine and uncontaminated by humanity's cruelties, a place where man could coexist with nature, not destroy it. Now murder had come to his own neck of the woods, staining the land with a good man's blood.

And he could do no more than take Jackson's murderer to the authorities. While leaving the killer's body on the mountain for carrion to feed on held a certain appeal, Sean knew the police would need to identify the attacker. But with snow coming, it might be days before anyone in an official capacity could reach the town. Once the weather socked in the remote mountain town of Kesky, the only transportation in or out was by dogsled.

Before he changed his mind and left the body to rot, Sean snaked out his hand toward the murderer's front pocket. What he'd assumed was a corpse snapped to a sitting position, yelled and swiped the knife at his gut.

Sean cursed and with a hunter's reflexes jerked aside, tumbling away from the weapon. While shock and grief had dulled Sean's senses, Jackson's murderer must have been gathering strength and waiting for the opportunity to attack. Sean had broken up enough fights among the miners to know this man was skilled in how to wield a knife or he would stab the weapon—not slice it. Off balance, Sean took a moment longer than he would have liked to recover and scramble upright.

Prepared and agile but unsteady on his feet, his opponent stood and shifted the knife to his right hand. In the dim light, the bloody weapon appeared almost black. The sneaky little bastard was threatening him with the same weapon he had used to murder Jackson.

Relishing his jacked-up senses, Sean felt his adrenaline pump. Without hesitation, he lunged forward, grasping for the attacker's wrist, grappling for control of the weapon. One quick twist of the captured wrist and the murderer dropped the knife to the dirt and would have spun away if not for Sean's tight grip.

With his free hand, the man reached into the pea-green jacket, no doubt intent on retrieving another weapon. Like hell would Sean allow that sneaky maneuver. He twisted the surprisingly delicate wrist harder, drawing a grunt of distress.

And received a sharp kick to his shin, an elbow jammed into the ribs. Sean ignored the biting pain. With grim determination, he hung on, using his superior strength and weight to wrestle the other man to the ground.

Together, they toppled, Sean landing on top of a wiry body, straining to escape. He estimated his opponent at five foot nine to five foot ten, no match for his conditioned six foot four. Still the shorter man struggled.

The jacket's hood fell back and sunny-gold hair spilled across the dirt. What the hell? His hot blood chilled. Sean flipped his opponent over and stared into the face of a woman with eyes as fierce and wary as a cornered fox.

Jackson's murderer was a woman?

The astonishing revelation of her gender caused him to loosen his grip. That's all she needed to take advantage. Strong, determined and clearly capable, she rolled away and kicked his feet out from under him. He fell hard, but not without grasping a handful of golden hair, trapping her beside him.

Panting furiously, she looked mad enough to spit bullets, confused enough to make a foolish mistake. She inched her hand inside her jacket.

"Don't even think it." He clamped his free hand over her wrist, imprisoning her.

She narrowed eyes that surged with green anger, bewilderment and a hint of fear. Now that he held her trapped, he expected her to plead, cry or beg forgiveness.

Instead she threatened him. "Assaulting a police officer is a federal offense."

"And what's murder?" he countered, not buying her claim of being an officer of the law for a milli-second.

"I didn't—"

"Lady, I walked into this cave and found you next to Jackson." He fought down the urge to shake her until the lies from her chapped lips ceased. Although she was strong for a female, her neck looked fragile, easy for him to snap. Fighting his own grief, anger and lust for revenge, he sought to tamp down his wildly surging emotions.

"That doesn't mean I killed him."

"The murder weapon was in *your* hand."

"Which hand?"

"The left."

She glanced at the blood-smeared cuff of her left sleeve. "I'm right-handed."

She sounded indignant at his accusation, but then what could he expect from a killer? He shrugged away his doubts. "The way you wield that knife, you're probably ambidextrous. No doubt you'd have liked to kill me, too."

Her voice was calm and even, as if accustomed to dealing with tough situations. "I wasn't trying to kill you."

"Really?" He didn't believe her story, not with the evidence right before his eyes.

"I came to and sat up. I didn't even know the knife was in my hand. Then you attacked." She stared at him as if she thought he was the one who was confused.

But he wouldn't be taken in so easily by her innocent demeanor. That's probably how she'd killed Jackson. He frowned and raised his voice. "You expect me to believe your flimsy explanation?"

At his harsh accusation, her entire body shuddered and slumped. Her eyes rolled to the top of her sockets.

Damn. Damn. Damn.

He wanted answers. And she'd either fainted on him or she was an excellent actress. Either way, Sean wasn't taking any chances. Without relinquishing his grip on her wrist, he perused Jackson's supplies.

A rabbit snare caught his eye. Perfect. Within moments he'd firmly tied the woman's hands behind her back. He supposed she wouldn't like her helpless position much once she came to and discovered that he'd trussed her like a goose—but she should have considered the consequences before she'd killed Jackson. Out here, men took care of their own.

Unwilling to risk any further unpleasant surprises, Sean unzipped her jacket and started to relieve her of the gun she'd reached for. He noted her curves with mechanical efficiency. What a waste. Unconscious, her features relaxed into an attractiveness he might have found appealing if they'd met under other circumstances.

She had unusually symmetrical features, wide-set eyes, angled cheekbones and lightly tanned skin framed by that lion's mane of golden hair. No wonder she'd taken poor Jackson by surprise. But Sean wouldn't let that angelic face fool him. His only interest in her womanly curves was to discover where she'd hidden the weapon she'd been so obviously reaching for.

He unzipped her jacket, parted the flap. Beneath her arm, she wore a shoulder harness with a sheathed gun clearly visible. He reached out to take the weapon.

She came to with a groan. Startled, he jerked his hand back, grazing her breast.

She stared at him accusingly—as if he were doing something wrong. "What are you…?"

He watched her arms strain as she discovered her tied wrists, noted the slight widening of her eyes that betrayed a hint of fear. He opened her jacket wider.

She flinched. "Don't!"

He could have reassured her. But a murderer didn't deserve courtesy. "I'm taking your gun—before you shoot me."

Her brows furrowed and a shadow hovered in her sea-green eyes. "Why would I want to shoot you?"

She spoke with such conviction he almost believed in her innocence. But he'd already seen her weapon. And she wouldn't distract him with clever questions. Reminding himself she was his prisoner, slowly and deliberately, he reached for her weapon. With her hands tied behind her, pulling her arms tight, her gun lay wedged between her arm and her breast. He slid his fingers over the handle of her gun, watching her stiffen as the back of his thumb touched the curve of her breast. He'd sensed how much she'd detested the brush of his fingers. Tough. Letting her keep the weapon wasn't an option. But he wouldn't take advantage of her helplessness, either. He would honor

Jackson by respecting what the old miner had taught him, and that homespun knowledge included acting the gentleman. He drew the gun out firmly, knowing she thought the worst of him, uncaring whether she believed he was about to harm her.

She'd taken his only family. She deserved to pay.

After checking her weapon to ensure the safety was on, he stuffed the gun into his jacket pocket. She watched him warily, only her ragged breathing revealing her fear. Starting beneath her arms, he patted her down, noting her lean waist, slender hips and long legs with trim ankles tucked into high-topped boots. By her clenched jaws, he surmised she was gritting her teeth, but she didn't utter a protest—not that it would have stopped him from searching for identification or another weapon.

He half expected her to attempt to kick him and remained alert. But although he could feel anger radiating off her, she remained stiff, unmoving.

When he reached her ankles, she rolled to her side. "Satisfied?"

Her question annoyed him. Who did she think she was to utter challenges? She could damn well answer *his* questions. He rocked back on his heels and stared at her. "Why did you kill Jackson?"

"Who's Jackson?" she countered with what appeared to be genuine puzzlement.

Sean resisted slamming his fist into her face. It wasn't in him to hurt a woman—no matter what she'd done. However, he had no intention of revealing that fact. He might extract more answers if she feared him. "Come on, lady. I don't have time to play twenty questions." He jerked her to her feet.

A moan broke from her tightly compressed lips and she slumped and would have fallen if he hadn't caught her. For her thin frame, she was surprisingly heavy. Remembering her strength, he realized she must be lean muscle.

Frowning, he eased her down onto Jackson's bedroll. "You hurt?"

She didn't answer but curled her legs under her and tried to scoot away from him like a wounded animal in a trap.

He pressed a firm hand to her shoulder. "Hold still, lady, before you do more damage."

"The name's Carlie. Carlie Myer."

Bill's wife? Stunned, Sean rocked back on his heels, suspicious as hell. She couldn't be Carlie Myer, could she? Two years ago, Bill had been one of Sean's best friends. They'd hunted and fished together, and Bill even owned a two percent share in the mine. Sean had been sorry when Bill had left Alaska and gone to Florida but was happy for his friend when he'd married a beautiful blond cop named Carlie and settled down.

Last year, Bill's death had hit him hard. He'd even written the widow a letter of condolence, but until today, Sean had never set eyes on Bill's wife.

And now both Jackson and Bill were dead.

Last time Sean had flown into town, he'd picked up a surprising message from his friend's widow. She'd wanted to visit him, so Sean had laid in supplies. Two weeks ago, he'd been expecting Carlie Myer's visit. In all the scenarios he'd played over in his mind about why she'd wanted to see him, he'd never imagined her turning up alone at the Dog

Mush. He'd expected her to come to Alaska to check out her inherited investment in the mine. When she hadn't shown up in Fairbanks on the prearranged date, he'd figured she'd changed her mind and stayed in Florida.

Now she'd arrived, literally out of nowhere. And finding her way into his neck of the mountains wasn't easy, especially for a woman born and bred in Florida's Suncoast. Perhaps she wasn't alone? Maybe an accomplice had run off into the woods and left her for dead. Warily he looked over his shoulder, but he spied nothing amiss.

Once more he reminded himself that if she was Carlie Myer, she was a cop and sworn to uphold the law. Bill had been a straight arrow, unlikely to hook up with a cold-blooded killer. Bill might have judged her incorrectly, but his friend had been keenly perceptive about people's characters. And just knowing this woman had been married to his friend made Sean question his previous conclusion that she was a murderer. Still, he'd found her with the knife in her hand.

She's your best friend's widow.

Yet minutes ago he'd been so sure she'd killed Jackson. He'd seen Jackson's blood on her left sleeve, the knife clenched in her fingers. The hard-packed floor of the mine gave him no sign that anyone else had or had not been here.

But she'd said she was right-handed.

So why was the blood on her left sleeve?

She's a cop.

Had she really tried to swipe him with the knife? Or had she sat up groggy the way she'd claimed, and before she'd gotten her bearings, he'd attacked? Sean was no longer certain. The facts didn't add up.

"How did you get here?" he asked. "Why did you kill the old prospector?"

Carlie didn't answer. Once again she'd slipped into unconsciousness. Had she been hurt in the fight with Jackson? Sean's suspicions might be diminishing but they didn't vanish. Two of his friends had encountered this woman—and both of them were dead. Still, he'd been so ready to blame her for Jackson's death, he hadn't checked to see if anyone else was near.

Perhaps both she and Jackson had been attacked. If she hadn't killed Jackson, then the person who had could be after her, too. The killer could be outside on the mountain, getting away even now.

Sean knelt beside her and covered her with a spare blanket. When she moaned and turned her head to the side, he spied blood and a nugget-sized bump three inches above the base of her neck, and he winced. So that's why she'd passed out. Had she sustained the injury while fighting Jackson? Or had someone else hit her? Either way, she probably had a concussion and shouldn't be left to sleep. He shook her shoulder, trying to wake her up. Not even one long eyelash fluttered. But the bleeding had almost stopped.

As he stood, his hand brushed a piece of plastic that must have slipped from her pocket during their struggle. Curious, he read the name on the driver's license. Carlie Myer. Bill's wife—no, widow, he corrected. Absently, he slipped her license into his pocket, pleased he'd confirmed her identity, but found it odd she carried no purse or backpack.

Sean considered untying her, believing he'd misjudged the woman. But first he'd look around.

Deciding there was little more he could do for Carlie until she awakened, Sean took more careful notice of the mine. Jackson's supplies, camp stove and tools were neatly stacked along one wall. Dishes cleaned and set out to dry from breakfast indicated the prospector had eaten alone.

Exiting the mine carrying Jackson's body, Sean knelt and gently set Jackson's body down. He searched the hard-packed earth but saw no signs of struggle, no footprints in the dirt. Normal sounds of the forest had returned. Arctic warblers fluttered in the willow thickets, crickets chirped and Dall sheep grazed in the high grasslands.

Through the first flutters of snow, he looked below to the town of Kesky, population one-hundred and two. They had a bank, a post office, a church, a grocery and hardware store and a one-roomed schoolhouse. In a town that size, a stranger would be noticed, especially an attractive woman. He doubted she'd passed through Kesky without being spotted. Had someone followed her up the mountain?

He and Jackson employed twenty men to work the main mine. None of the miners would have allowed Carlie to make the rough climb to the Dog Mush unescorted. Maybe she'd come up with Jackson. But why?

Unfortunately, she hadn't divulged in her letter the reason she'd been so intent on coming to see Sean.

When she awakened, he intended to get some answers.

He returned to the cave, lit an oil lamp and examined the unconscious woman again. She displayed no other signs of injury. Her face was unnaturally pale, but neither cut nor bruised. Her chest rose and fell with rhythmic precision, and from the way she'd fought, he doubted she had any broken limbs.

She let out another groan and turned onto her side, tilting her neck at an odd angle. Hoping her sole injury was the bump on her head, Sean did his best to make her more comfortable, untying her hands, folding a blanket to pillow her head.

He should have known Bill wouldn't have let himself be hogtied by anyone less than a beauty. But did those lush lips and dark eyelashes hide a mystery that could get a man killed?

Staring at her wouldn't give him the answers he needed. Nevertheless, he felt compelled to study her lightly tanned skin, her straight, no-nonsense nose and lips that hinted at passion. No wonder his friend had fallen in love and married so quickly.

Sean forced his gaze away. Although he wasn't hungry, he primed and lit Jackson's stove and set water on it for coffee to boil, again wondering why she had come to Alaska to see him.

He'd have to be patient until she could tell him. Sean knew how to be patient. He could track an animal for miles. He could spend months working a vein in the mine. He could certainly wait for the answers this woman could supply.

He had no doubts she'd had a rough time. And

with that knot on her head, no doubt when Carlie awakened she'd have one hell of a headache.

A cool gust whipped around the corner and into the cave, and Sean shivered as if a dark cloud clutched at him. Shaking off the eerie portent, he added coffee to the pot. He wouldn't let his grief or his temper or his heart rule his decisions. He'd keep an open mind until he possessed the facts. Pondering over the best way to learn the truth, his gaze again turned to the unconscious woman. One way or another, she was going to tell him exactly what had happened—if she ever woke up.

Chapter Two

Carlie's head pounded and pain stabbed behind her eyes, yet a sense of urgency forced her to open her eyelids. She needed to… She had to… Had to what?

Where the hell was she? She lay on a sleeping bag inside a fair-sized cave. The mouth-watering scent of coffee tantalized her stomach, which made embarrassingly loud noises.

"How's the head?"

At the sound of a deep baritone, she craned her neck. Pain shot down from her nape to her back. She gasped and fought through the swirling tunnel of blackness to study the man hovering over her.

Although he'd asked how she felt, he didn't look particularly concerned. Actually, he leaned aggressively forward, straining the fabric of his shirt, appearing as if he couldn't decide whether to help her or hit her, but perhaps that was because he was blurry around the edges. She closed her eyes, took a deep breath, then opened them again, willing herself to focus. This time he came in as clear and crisp as a focused camera lens. The combination of his gray-eyed stare, harsh cheekbones and five-o'clock shadow caused her to tremble. Even his thin lips drawn in a tight line seemed judgmental and disapproving.

She had never seen him before. Who was he?

She tried to sit up and discovered her wrists were numb. Clenching and unclenching her fingers, she forced the blood back into them. After flexing her arms, she realized her gun had been removed from her holster, and a sinking sensation in the pit of her stomach kicked in. A cop never gave up her weapon.

Something was wrong. And it wasn't just the odd circumstance she'd found herself in. She was wearing ugly boots, a heavily padded olive jacket and khaki slacks. And cold seeped through her thermal underwear into her bones. Thermal underwear? Where had that thought come from? Her eyes widened as a flurry of snow fluttered just behind the strange man. *Snow!* It didn't snow in Tampa, Florida.

"What happened? Who are you? Where am I?"

His eyes, as enigmatic as a wolf's, darkened. "I already told you—"

"You did?" His words implied they'd already had a conversation. She drew an unsteady breath and tried to remember, but the pain in her head was taking its toll. Why didn't she know this man? Lord, with those hard gray eyes and the lightning rush of her pulse whenever he looked at her, she didn't know how she could have forgotten him. He had a fierce way of staring that made her feel like he was sizing her up as prey. Yet he held so still, and she sensed if she made one wrong move, he would pounce.

Damn it. Why couldn't she remember?

She and Harry, her partner, must have been working a case that had gone down wrong, but she couldn't recall any details, and a tight knot slowly formed in her stomach. "We've met before?"

One eyebrow cocked in skepticism. "You don't remember me?" he asked very deliberately. "I'm Sean McCabe."

His icy flash of doubt annoyed her as much as it confused her. "Carlie Brandon."

"Brandon?" He shook his head and let out a long, low whistle of disbelief. "There's no need to lie. I'll try and help if I can."

Lie? She'd told him the truth. The knot tightened another notch. Yet, despite her memory loss she tried to remain calm. Maybe he wasn't the enemy.

In the haunting gray light of the cave, she could see a tight expression on his lips, and she realized he'd told her almost nothing about her situation. He seemed tense, a leashed force of taut muscles primed to spring if she made the wrong move. As a frisson of dread swept through her, she fought to keep the rising fear from her voice. "Could I have some water, please?"

When he didn't hesitate to pour water from a canteen into a tin cup, she sagged against the sleeping bag, relieved. He didn't seem to want to mistreat her. And when her numb fingers couldn't hold the cup, he raised it to her lips with a hand that looked as if it had spent a long time in the wilderness. She'd always noticed a man's hands. Indicating he worked with them for a living, his hands were large, the palms and pads of his fingers callused, the fingers long and without adornment. But then she didn't need the lack of a ring to tell her this man wasn't married. She couldn't imagine any circumstance where he would share himself with a woman.

Although he eyed her steadily, he seemed uncomfortable around her, as if unsure whether to treat her with consideration or hostility. Her injury and weakness seemed to irritate him almost as much as it did her.

The water was cold, surprisingly refreshing, as if it had come straight from the refrigerator. She doubted politeness would soften him up. Still, she tried. ''Thanks.''

Her words had no more effect on him than they had on the rocky walls around her. Still, she was aware of his intense scrutiny, the subtle aura of power he radiated as he completed the ordinary task of screwing the cap back onto the canteen and tossing it onto a pile of camping gear.

''I need to know what happened here.'' His voice echoed darkly in the tomblike chamber. ''Why don't you tell me your real name—for starters.''

At his words, confusion settled in the pit of her gut. He acted as if he was giving her a test, as if he knew her name and that she'd been lying to him. Had a lunatic taken her captive? He'd said he'd help, had given her water, then sharpened his tone as if she were a habitual liar. For all she remembered, he could have been the one who'd caused the pounding at the base of her skull.

Her inability to recall her circumstances wasn't just inconvenient but downright alarming. She didn't recognize the partially covered body just outside the cave. Most likely, she'd been working a case and ended up here, but she hadn't an inkling where *here* was or of how to play out her situation. Worse, her partner might be just around the bend, either hurt or injured, and depending on her to get them out of here.

Why couldn't she remember? "I'm not lying. I have identification in my…"

But she wasn't in uniform. Wild, speculative thoughts coursed through her. She must have been drugged. Taken somewhere. She reminded herself that Harry must be looking for her. If she could just stay alive, help would arrive. She swallowed hard and forced her gaze to the man looming over her. He looked hard and about two seconds away from doing her bodily harm.

Dizzy from the pounding headache, she was in no condition to fight. Actually, even if she'd been perfectly healthy, she would have been no match for two-hundred-plus pounds of lean, angry muscle. So she had no intention of provoking his anger.

Her mouth was still dry, but she was reluctant to ask for more water, preferring that he keep his distance. "What do you want with me?"

With a don't-mess-with-me look, he set down the cup beside her and folded his arms across his broad chest. "I want answers."

"Don't we all."

He jerked his thumb toward the mouth of the cave, at the body beneath a blanket. A bloody knife lay next to it. "Why did you kill my partner, Jackson?"

She hadn't killed anyone. Or at least she didn't think she had. Her mom had always told her the best defense was a strong offense, so at his accusation, she came out swinging. "How do I know *you* didn't kill him?"

"The man was like a father to me. Besides, I'm not the one with blood on my sleeve."

As his words sank in, she glanced down at her sleeve to the dark stain and shivered.

He was accusing her of...murder. Her mind couldn't wrap around the thought. Murder? Oh, God. Why couldn't she remember? If only the pounding behind her eyes would diminish, she might think more clearly.

Like an expert interrogator, he gave her no time to recuperate from his allegation. "And before you lie and tell me you didn't kill him, you might want to consider that I saw the bloody knife in your hand."

She had to concentrate, but a black hole in her memory seemed to have sucked away every recollection. "I can't remember."

"How convenient, *Ms. Brandon.*"

He seemed to emphasize her last name with a mocking tone, then wait for her reaction. But how was she supposed to react? She'd told him the truth. She was born Carlie May Brandon and she'd never married, never gone by another name. Had she been working this case undercover and used an alias? But Carlie didn't do undercover. She was just a uniformed officer who patrolled the streets. Her gaze strayed to the body and skittered away. What had happened?

Think.

The last moment she recalled was stopping a speeder on the causeway connecting Tampa and St.

Petersburg. Harry had teased her about letting off the cute guy in the Corvette with just a warning. It had been Tuesday, around 5:00 p.m.

"What day is this?" she asked.

Sean didn't seem surprised she'd lost track of the days; his expression didn't change one iota. But then, he looked as if he were carved from the same unforgiving rock that formed mountains. Beneath his full-length parka, he wore a black wool shirt, heavy denim pants and sturdy hiking boots. From his heavy clothing, the cold climate and the camping gear in the cave, she guessed they were in the mountains, someplace up north or out west. Colorado or Canada, maybe.

Wherever she was, time didn't seem to have much meaning. She didn't hear the sounds of civilization. No cars, no trains. No police sirens indicating help on the way. Obviously she wasn't in Florida anymore and could only count on her own resources.

The man standing over her was a formidable opponent. Yet he didn't seem the usual street criminal. Intelligence gleamed from his eyes, and the set of his mountainous shoulders warned her of his self-control. She doubted she could incite him into making mistakes.

At least he was talking to her. "It's Saturday," he told her.

She'd lost four days. Four days. "You're sure?"

"Very. It's October 30."

She blinked when he added the year. No way. He had to be trying to trick her. But his words had been so offhand, downright casual. And what reason would he have to lie? She swallowed hard and tried for a normal tone. ''Are you sure?''

He cocked his head, his deep baritone suspicious. ''Lose a day?''

Stunned, she blinked hard, fighting back tears. ''Near as I can tell, I've lost over two years.''

Two years gone, vanished as if she'd never lived them. She had to stay calm, in control of her rising panic. The knock on her head could have caused a temporary memory loss. Surely her memory would return if she just concentrated hard enough.

Ignoring his eyebrows raised in disbelief was easy while thoughts raced through her head like a runaway train. What was wrong with her? It was as if she'd never lived the last two years. Panic surged through her. She had no idea where she was or how she'd gotten here. Suppose her memories never returned? Suppose she *had* killed Jackson?

Fear clamped around her chest and squeezed. At least she'd retained most of her memories. She remembered her family, her friends, her job. But she'd lost two whole years. And she'd awakened in a cave and been accused of murder. She suspected no one would believe her memory loss, and even if they did, they might lock her up and toss away the—

Stop it. You're a trained professional. Act like one. Focus on the facts.

She wasn't completely helpless. She had a real sense of who she was, a cop—not a murderer. If she'd killed Jackson, she must have done so in self-defense. But even as a cop, she'd never had cause to pull her gun.

Still, a lot could have changed in two years. Perhaps she'd made detective or gone into undercover work.

While she remained silent, Sean McCabe stared at her as if waiting for her to admit she'd lied about the partial amnesia. His acute stare told her he was taking her lack of memory personally, and like a dog gnawing a juicy steak bone, he wasn't about to let her go until he was satisfied.

She wished she *could* lie, because that would mean she was in possession of her full memory. All her recent recollections were gone—more than twenty-four months' worth. Trying to force a memory only made her head ache worse. Gingerly she touched the knot. Perhaps when the swelling receded, her memories would return.

Her partial amnesia could have been worse. After all, she remembered her name, her childhood and her parents. She had a job with the police department, a family that loved her and many friends. All she needed to do was find a phone, and even if her memories never returned, they could fill her in.

Slowly her speeding heart calmed. She was alive, and at the moment her accuser didn't seem inclined to hurt her. She wasn't even sure if she was being held hostage, but if so, perhaps she could escape.

If his intentions were honorable, if he thought she'd murdered his friend, why hadn't he called the police? She stared back into the darkened eyes surveying her with a mixture of pity and bridled anger and wondered if revealing her memory loss had been a mistake.

His tone was low, harsh. "Tell me what you remember."

"About what?" she asked, vowing to give him nothing he could use against her.

"About…us."

"Us?" That one word rocked her, hinting at a former and possibly a current personal relationship. Although his mountain-man ruggedness was attractive, she was positive they couldn't be lovers. She felt no connection to him, could dredge up no past feelings about him one way or the other. And yet, a certain awareness zinged through her every time she looked at him. She noticed the way his eyes softened around the edges every time she winced in pain, the way he jutted his jaw at a certain angle when he didn't get the answers that he sought, the way he held his back to Jackson's body, as if keeping the man out of sight would lessen the pain of his loss. But as for real memory, for all she knew, she'd never met Sean McCabe before she'd awakened and told him her name was Carlie Brandon.

Thoughts swirling in a muddy haze of confusion, she'd never felt at such a disadvantage. Her lack of knowledge undermined her normal confidence. Confused and hurting, she wanted to close her eyes and sleep until the pain receded.

"Do you remember fighting with Jackson?" he asked softly, too softly, more than a hint of menace and resolve in his tone.

She rubbed her pounding temple, wishing she didn't feel so vulnerable, wishing for her gun. "I don't remember fighting with anyone."

"And no one else is here with you?"

She forced her eyes to stay open. At least Sean was considering the possibility that someone else may have killed Jackson. While thankful for his ability to focus on facts, what she really wanted was his trust. She sensed that once this man made up his mind, he would pursue his goal no matter how difficult the challenge.

She wanted him on her side and decided to use every ounce of her persuasive abilities to prove her innocence. Right now, it would be wonderful if he believed her, but she'd settle for what she could get. "The first thing I remember is you asking how my head felt. I don't know where I am or how I got here."

"You're in Alaska."

"Alaska!" She sat up abruptly and pain sliced down her neck.

"Easy." With a big hand on each of her shoulders, he steadied her.

He smelled of cedar and a hint of wood smoke. For a moment she thought he might insist she lie back down. Instead he held her until she stopped swaying and she took comfort in his support. In her injured state, the last thing she needed was to crack her head again. She accepted his help, and yet she sensed the crackling tension in him. Obviously he wanted to find answers to Jackson's murder as badly as she did.

While she couldn't be certain whether to trust him, she'd come to the conclusion Sean McCabe would not act with haste. No matter how deep his feelings, he was a man with unusual self-control.

"I don't remember how I got here. I'm from Florida."

Her head spun. Her stomach refused to settle. And

she wished he'd stop staring at her as if she were an exotic animal in a zoo. "How do we know each other?"

Before he answered, voices and several dog barks from outside the cave interrupted. A new voice echoed through the cave. "Sean! You want us to bring the sleds into the mine or leave them out—"

Three men entered the cave. The first man was huge as a grizzly bear and looked as if he'd never used a razor. His black beard must have been a foot long. He towered over a slender youth who wore neon-green ski gear, goggles on his forehead and five earrings in his left ear. The third man looked ordinary enough, except when he scowled at her, she spotted a gold front tooth.

From somewhere in her mind came a saying about women searching for husbands in a state where men outnumbered women eight to one. *The odds were good but the goods were odd.* Even with the knot on her head she couldn't have dreamed up an odder assortment of men.

All three visitors took in Jackson's body beneath the blanket and then their hostile gazes settled on her. At the anger and accusations in their faces, she wanted to lie back down and close her eyes, but she forced herself to remain sitting upright.

The man with the long beard pointed at her and spoke with a harsh growl. "Marvin said my brother killed his murderer."

No wonder the man eyed her with such hostility. He was Jackson's brother. Automatically, she looked for a similarity in features—but she had no idea what the man she'd supposedly killed looked like.

As if sympathetic to her plight, Sean placed himself between her and the intruders and sat on a crate by the camp stove. "I was mistaken, Roger."

"Hell of a mistake," chided the man with the gold tooth. "We could have all walked into a trap."

Carlie kept quiet, her gaze flickering from the other men to Sean, who'd clearly taken charge. He had a stillness about him, a calm that spread outward from his center, which reassured her.

But Roger, Jackson's brother, was clearly incensed. And while the gold-toothed fellow seemed to find her predicament diverting, the twenty-something kid in the ski clothes looked none too happy with her, either.

The kid tossed his goggles to the ground and unzipped his ski jacket. "Want me to call—"

"Why bring in outsiders?" Roger muttered through his beard as he peered at her with a scowl. "We should string her up right now."

The man with the gold front tooth turned his head and spit out a stream of tobacco juice. "I'm not hanging no female."

"There will be no vigilante justice on this mountain," Sean said with an authority that sliced through the argument and had the men looking at their feet. "If she killed Jackson, she'll get the justice she deserves."

The men settled around the stove, forming a circle that closed her out, their argument swirling around her like a tornado. Amid the shouts, an aura of great stillness surrounded Sean. He did not shout. He did not shift from foot to foot or clench his fingers. And he didn't just take up space, he controlled it.

Exhausted, she lay back in the blankets, bunching the material in her fists. Sean appeared to be in charge and inclined to protect her from the others.

But who would protect her from him?

AFTER TYLER UNZIPPED his ski jacket, he poured coffee, and Sean glanced at Carlie. Although he caught an alert gleam of speculation in her expression, the effort to hold up her head was costing her. Fatigue crept in around the edges of her eyes and her mouth drew into a tight line of pain. She'd clenched her jaw, but after she caught him watching her, she'd forced her features to relax, as if admitting to pain was a weakness. He couldn't help but admire her mettle. She was strong, this woman, and he'd long ago discovered that strength often hid powerful passions. He couldn't help wondering what kind of passions simmered beneath her surface. He also wondered if she thought she'd told him the truth.

She required medical treatment, but first, he had to think of the best way to calm down Roger. Jackson's brother had one hell of a temper. He loved nothing better than a good fight. Next to fighting, he liked shouting, but once he settled, he had a good heart. And he never held a grudge.

Sean wished he could have a few moments alone with the man. From his clenched fists to the tight cords in his neck, Jackson's brother appeared as if the grief bottled up inside him was ready to burst. But short of a fistfight, Sean had no way to ease Roger's grief, fearing even a few kind words might set off Roger in front of the others.

Tyler set the coffee back on the stove, but not

before shooting Carlie a look of angry speculation. He, too, had liked and respected Jackson, who had been popular among the men, not just because he was an old-timer and one of the partners in the Dog Mush, but because he had the habit of adopting strays, the lost, the lonely, the forgotten. So even the irreverent Tyler held him in high esteem, and his anger at his murderer was fully justified in his eyes.

Sean next glanced at Marvin. His normally gold-smiling visage was tight, as if having difficulty holding his poker face. Sean had his work cut out for him to defuse the men's anger. Carlie was a stranger; Kesky's inhabitants held a natural distrust of outsiders that was common in small towns and more prevalent in the Alaskan wilds.

Not liking the way all three men glared at Carlie and fearing their hostility could erupt into violence, Sean squatted back on his heels and accepted a cup of coffee. "When I called Marvin, I thought she—" he jerked his thumb at Carlie "—was dead, too."

"Too bad you were wrong." Roger's dark brows drew together as he stared at his brother's body.

"Why did she kill Jackson?" Marvin asked, his gambler's eyes assessing Carlie with an interest that made Sean's protective urges kick in.

"She isn't going to tell," Tyler said with a superior smirk that he probably thought made him appear worldly but instead revealed a hurt young man trying to be brave after the recent loss of his father in a hunting accident. "I'll bet she's claiming she didn't even do it."

"I'm not sure she did," Sean said. At his words,

the woman relaxed her body and eased her head back onto the sleeping bag.

Roger finally broke the tense silence. "Care to explain that, boss?"

Three pairs of male eyes locked on Sean as if he had the cabin fever that makes a man insane after spending too long indoors during winter. They all needed time to look at the murder more rationally. Calmly, he sipped his too-hot coffee, relishing the liquid as it burned his tongue.

"Those pretty eyes are playing havoc with your thinking," Marvin said before Sean replied. "There wasn't nobody up here except the old man and the girl. Who else could have done in Jackson?"

"There isn't anyone else here *now,*" Sean stated with cool logic. "But suppose someone attacked both of them?"

"What are you implying?" Roger asked.

"When I first came into the cave, she looked dead. Maybe our killer made the same mistake."

"Jeez." Tyler shook his head in disgust. "I'm not believing my ears."

"Is that what she said?" Eyes narrowing, Roger clenched and unclenched his fist.

Sean kept his gaze on the men, yet he was very aware of the woman on the sleeping bag. She'd been remarkably quiet during their discussion, not once interrupting to defend herself. He couldn't fault her judgment and he respected her ability to realize that right now, remaining silent was the better part of valor. If she moved so much as an inch, they'd know it. But she wasn't trying to escape. Instead she stared at him with pain-filled eyes edged with hope.

He softened his tone. "Look, all I'm saying is that Carlie was injured, too. Other possibilities exist. And I want to look into all of them."

Tyler nodded. "That's a good idea."

"You aren't the law," Marvin challenged Sean without quite meeting his eyes.

"I should be in charge," Roger muttered. "He was my brother."

Sean ignored the interruptions. "Jackson practically raised me from a boy. I want to find his killer just as badly as you, maybe more. But I refuse to jump to any hasty conclusions."

"Seems to me you're jumping over backward to give the pretty lady the benefit of the doubt," Roger complained.

Roger should know better. Jackson's brother was well aware of Sean's debt to the old prospector. He'd never forget Jackson's patience as the man taught him to trap, hunt and solve word problems for school. When a restless boy had complained of homework, it was Jackson who had explained the value of an engineering degree, who helped Sean focus on the future instead of dwelling on the past. Sean would never forget the love Jackson had freely given to a homeless boy. Nor would he forget that Jackson deserved justice.

"She's even got blood on her sleeve," Marvin added. "What more proof of murder do you need?"

Tyler pointed rudely at Carlie. "What don't we let her speak for herself?"

Sean stared the kid down. "She has a knot on her head the size of a goose egg. And she can't remember anything that happened."

Tyler's eyes widened. "Wow! You're saying she's got amnesia?"

"How convenient," Marvin muttered. "Ten to one, she did it."

"We're not betting on a poker game here," Sean admonished him.

"You believe her?" Tyler's boyish voice rose an octave, indicating how upset he'd become as the news of another death sank in. After his own father's accident, Tyler had become close to Jackson, often tagging along as the old miner hiked the mountain. Tyler would don his skis and tear down the slope with daredevil enthusiasm.

"Yes." Sean held Tyler's stare. "I'm inclined to believe her."

Tyler dropped his gaze and blinked away a tear. "Mind telling us why, boss?"

Actually Sean minded a lot. He didn't want to reveal Carlie's identity and that she was Bill's widow.

If Carlie hadn't killed Jackson, then the person who had could be after her, too. Sean had known Bill's work for customs was dangerous, had speculated the car accident that had taken his life might not have been an accident. During Bill's assignment in Alaska, the men had fished, hunted and shared stories around a campfire. But Bill had been close-mouthed about his cases and now Sean wished he knew more. In fact, how did he know that Bill's murderer hadn't followed Carlie to Alaska to kill her, too? Jackson may have simply been in the wrong place at the wrong time.

Until the real killer was apprehended, Carlie

wasn't safe. Sean needed to keep her where he could watch over her, but how? He felt an obligation to protect his friend's widow until they learned the truth. He owed Bill his life. When a wall of the mine had collapsed, a timber had trapped Sean. With his air running out, he wouldn't have survived—but at risk to his own life, Bill had crawled back, dug him out with his bare hands, pried off the timber and saved him from suffocation.

Sean always paid his debts.

But how could he protect Carlie if the authorities took her away to Fairbanks? He wanted her close by until she recovered her memory. She had no reason to trust him, a stranger, and he didn't believe she would stay with him willingly. And he needed to keep her identity secret, even from his friends in this small town where rumor spread faster than bear grease.

An idea suddenly popped into his mind. "I was hoping you all would give the lady—"

"She ain't no lady," Marvin protested.

Tyler turned on Marvin. "Let the man finish his sentence, will you?"

Sean stood and hooked his fingers into his belt. "We'll give her our protection until we find out the truth. Jackson's killer might be after her, too."

"That's some story you're expecting us to swallow," Roger muttered.

"There's something I haven't told you boys," Sean said, lowering his voice to appear as if he was taking them into his confidence.

"Well, don't keep us in the dark. Tell us." Tyler's tone rose, revealing his eagerness to hear a secret.

While Sean glanced out of the corner of his eye at Carlie, he did his best to keep his voice steady. "I want you to give her the benefit of the doubt."

"But why?" Roger prodded.

"Because on my last trip into the city, we married. The lady's my wife."

Chapter Three

His wife?

They were married? Sean's announcement stunned Carlie speechless as the men carried Jackson's body down a steep trail. Although she'd suggested leaving the body in the mine until a homicide detective investigated the crime scene, Sean had informed her animals would get to the body before the authorities could arrive. So they'd packed Jackson onto a sled, and Carlie tried not to think about the murdered man. Instead she considered Sean's claim that they were husband and wife.

The men's silence in the pine forest was broken only by the slide of falling rocks, the crunch of leaves, snaps of twigs underfoot and the occasional masculine grunt. Buffeted by a heavy head wind and flanked by sheer rock walls, the trail—consisting of icy sheets and compacted snowdrifts alternating with steep dirt patches—was not conducive to asking questions.

But Carlie couldn't resist glancing at Sean McCabe, who claimed to be her husband. He walked with the grace of a mountain cat and was just as unapproachable. For a man who was supposed to be her spouse, he hadn't exhibited much sympathy toward her plight. His face, all harsh planes and angles, never turned her way. And yet, behind his mask of indifference, she sensed his keen interest in her.

What kind of husband was he?

From the first time she'd awakened, he'd accused her of murder. Why would a husband think the worst of his wife? And he'd given no indication then they had a personal relationship, treating her as if they were strangers. Nor had he given her explanations about the two years she couldn't remember.

To be fair and give him credit, although he was still grieving over Jackson, he *had* defended her from the other men's aggression.

He had helped her.

But she expected more from a man to whom she had committed to spend the rest of her life; he had to back her no matter how suspicious her circumstances.

But he had.

He hadn't, however, gone out of his way to reassure her; not by a glance or a squeeze of the hand had he indicated he was more than a casual acquaintance.

While she couldn't remember him, she'd assumed her marriage would contain a certain intimacy, a bonding greater than other relationships. She must have loved him if she'd married this man. But even if her memories were gone and she couldn't recall her own feelings, why couldn't she find any evidence of *his* feelings for her?

He must have been shocked when she couldn't

remember him, more shocked to find her next to the dead body of his adoptive father with the murder weapon in hand. Although he'd been grieving, he hadn't acted shocked, he'd spoken clearly, concisely and taken charge right off the bat. But still…a husband should always support his wife. What kind of man had she married?

A small slab of snow broke loose and shot down a gully, reminding her she'd awakened in another world. Where had she met Sean? She must have loved him to distraction to have moved to Alaska, left her family and given up a job she loved. She felt awful that she couldn't remember their first dance, first kiss or making love. Knowing they must have shared these intimacies as man and wife, she had difficulty reconciling her husband with the man who'd recently accused her of murder. No matter how often she searched his flinty stare, she could find no display of tenderness or affection. Right now, she'd settle for just a little familiarity.

But he seemed as forbidding as the mountain's summit. And just as hard to reach.

They strode past alders, willows and pine, and she took the opportunity to observe him. Sure, his body appealed to her. Who wouldn't be attracted to those mountainous shoulders tapering to a lean waist and narrow hips? Nor would she deny her fascination with how the northern sunlight played off the angles of his tanned skin. His black hair was cut short in a style she found attractive. But the outside was just window dressing. And looking at him gave her few clues to his thoughts.

Frustrated by her lack of memory, she peeked

down to the one-street town below. A church squatted next to a few stores. Cabins, chimneys curling wispy smoke into the blue sky, dotted the steep landscape. She figured the town couldn't have a population of more than a hundred people, and if the town was anything like Riverview where she lived, folks knew one another's business. Likely some of these people would have attended their wedding and the town paper would have published the story.

So why didn't either Roger or Marvin or the college-age kid named Tyler know she was Sean's wife? While Sean's announcement had left her breathless and shocked, Roger's jaw had dropped, his pink lips peeking through his thick beard. Marvin's eyes had gone wide. Only Tyler had simply cocked an eyebrow and taken the news in stride.

Their reactions piqued her suspicions. Not only didn't they recognize her as Sean's wife, they didn't appear to know that Sean had married.

Yet she couldn't deny the wedding ring beneath her glove. During the last two years, she must have met Sean, fallen in love and married. But the only emotion she could dredge up whenever she looked at him was curiosity and tingling awareness of his presence.

Just past head-high willows, the trail ahead widened and forked. With no discussion among them, Sean sent the three men with Jackson's body down the right path of the mountain and gestured for her to follow him to the left.

Ice covered the steeper part of the trail, but Sean walked without concern, his feet steady. Silent, like a hunter. No twigs snapped beneath his feet. His clothing didn't rustle. He moved as one with the mountain, quickly, quietly, methodically.

While he seemed at ease in the silence, she could no longer hold back her maelstrom of questions. "Where are we going?"

"To my cabin."

She halted in her tracks, didn't bother masking the suspicion in her tone. "*Your* cabin. If we're married, don't I live there, too?"

"You will now." He kept walking in that steady stride that could eat up miles.

Her annoyance rising, she hurried to keep up. Was he deliberately being obtuse? How could she have married such a poor communicator?

She caught up, tugged on his arm, drawing him to a stop. "Do we or do we not live together?"

She didn't like the way her words came out breathless, but blamed it on the lack of oxygen in the high altitude and not his stare or the full force of his personality hitting her squarely and making her feel jumpy. At the intensity on his face, she wanted to take a step backward. But hell could freeze over before she'd let him think he could intimidate her.

"It might be better if you remembered on your own." His voice sounded reasonable.

"Better for whom?" she countered, her temper rising. "Look, mister, I appreciate you keeping your friends from stringing me up from the nearest tree, but I don't know you from squat."

"Are you in the habit of marrying strangers?" he teased, a gleam in his eyes softening his face.

"Obviously I've picked up some bad habits."

"I've been called worse."

"Now, why don't I find that hard to believe?" she muttered, wondering how he'd changed the subject so smoothly. But she refused to let him distract her. "If you're my husband, then start acting like it. I want some answers and I'd like them now. Please."

"My cabin…our cabin," he corrected himself, "is around the next bend. We can talk there."

He set off without waiting for her agreement, once again leaving her to either tag along after him or not. Her blood sizzled at his refusal to answer simple questions. For a moment she considered hiking back to where the trails separated and heading into town and the nearest phone.

But Marvin, Tyler and Roger had gone ahead with Jackson's body. She shuddered at the welcome she imagined they would give her if she showed up alone. Her other alternative was to remain here and freeze—not too appealing. The sun had begun a rapid descent behind the mountain's summit, shadows lengthened and the temperature dropped ten degrees. She could only guess how cold the night would become, and not even her hot temper would keep her warm.

Furious, she stomped off after Sean, slipped around a bend and almost bumped into him. He didn't appear the least bit sheepish or surprised to be caught waiting for her.

Placing his hands on her shoulders, he steadied her. "Slow down. This last stretch is the steepest."

He didn't exaggerate. The trail took a forty-five-degree bend downward. The remains of last winter's snow had compacted into a sheet of ice and clung to the mountainside. If he hadn't waited for her, she might have tumbled down the steep incline face-first.

"I don't want you to open up that knot on your head."

"Thanks."

Maybe a hard fall would knock some sense into her. Or better still, bring her memories back. She had no business traipsing down the mountainside alone. Carlie was a city girl—the closest she got to camping was the Holiday Inn. But then Sean would know of her limited ability to survive in the wild, so he had no business leaving her to fend for herself. A bear could get her.

Before she lost hold of her temper once again, she forced herself to think. Maybe she'd learned some new wilderness skills in the last two years and had now forgotten them. She couldn't keep making assumptions as if those two years hadn't happened and then blame Sean for treating her for the tenderfoot she had been and now was again.

Besides, she had other problems to worry about. She'd been accused of murder. Sean's cabin might end up being more prison than sanctuary, and it was only a matter of time before the authorities placed her under arrest.

She gazed up into his face, searched his eyes that flickered with a glint of humor amid the concern, and sensed he would treat her fairly. He wouldn't let a mob string her up. She'd be safe with him.

With no warning, Sean yanked her against him, pulled her off balance and toppled backward toward the ledge.

"Hey—"

Her protest died in her throat as he locked his arms around her back so tightly, she had difficulty drawing a breath. With the force of a tidal wave, he hurled them over the precipice.

She braced for a jolting crash, but they landed with only a minor bump. But they were sliding. Sliding.

Wind whistled in her ears. Hair wrapped around her eyes, blocking her vision. Had he gone crazy, throwing himself over the cliff's edge and taking her with him? Was he trying to kill her?

Rational thought fled as she shook her face free of her hair, and when she could see again, she gasped in terror. Although Sean had taken the weight of the fall on his back and she'd landed on top of him, they shot down the mountain, gathering speed with no visible way of stopping. Headfirst and chest to chest, they slid down the icy peak, skidding dangerously close to large rocks and pine stumps, generating miniature avalanches and rock slides.

Desperately she searched for a handhold to slow or halt their mad fall. But her grasping fingers felt nothing but loose rock and icy snow.

Fifty yards down hill, a huge boulder stood in their path. They'd never survive a head-on collision.

"Roll!" Carlie ordered, grabbing his jacket and twisting as hard as she could to the right, taking Sean with her into a spiral. Corkscrewing down the mountain, they rolled over and over, plunging and bumping ever downward.

Forced to shut her eyes to avoid ice, pebbles and forest debris, Carlie clung to Sean and prayed for a gradual stop. When they bounced into thin air, her stomach lurched.

They landed with a thud that tore them apart.

She slid on her side for an instant before she realized somehow she'd done a one-eighty-degree turn and now was pitching downward feet first.

Sean had also turned around and skidded below her. But the path had gone right. They both were falling straight toward a cliff so steep, she couldn't even see where they would land.

With the last of her strength, she dug in her heels, slowing her momentum. But not enough.

Even worse, it appeared as if Sean had managed to stop his mad slide. She was about to run into him and knock them both to their deaths.

She tried to fling her body to one side, would have succeeded, but a hand clamped over her ankle, jerking her to a stop a mere ten feet before the cliff's edge. For a full minute she just lay on her back, staring straight up into the darkening sky and appreciating her every breath.

Sean lightly squeezed her ankle. "You okay?"

"Just dandy."

She took a mental inventory. Her hands and feet, knees and elbows all seemed to be in working order. She thanked her lucky stars they'd landed on one of the huge patches of ice and snow that clung to the mountain's north face.

"You sure?"

"Oh sure, I'm fine. It's just the usual boring day in the life of Carlie Brandon. I wake up to find I'm practically at the North Pole, two years of my life are missing and I'm married to a man I don't recognize. As if that's not enough to deal with, my darling husband accuses me of murder and then…for no apparent reason, he throws me off a cliff.''

''I had a reason.'' He turned on his side to look at her, the husky timbre of his voice deepening.

''Care to share it with me?''

''A red circle of laser light centered on your temple.''

He'd thought someone was trying to kill her. ''So you decided to save me by hurling me over a cliff. You couldn't have told me to duck?''

His lips twitched at her sarcasm but his amusement never reached his gray eyes. ''Someone was sighting a gun at your head. Ducking wouldn't have taken you out of the line of fire.''

She frowned, tried hard to recall one tiny fact from the last two years that could give her a clue to who wanted her dead, but came up with zip. Instead, she concentrated on her current predicament. She hadn't seen any red dot of light. ''I didn't hear a shot.''

He climbed to his feet and shook snow from his hair and collar. ''That doesn't mean someone wasn't out to get you.''

She lay on her back looking up at him. Had he saved her life? Or recklessly endangered it? Since he'd gone down the mountain with her, placing his own life in jeopardy, she was inclined to believe him.

He reached down and helped her to her feet. His hand was warm, strong, gentle. But he released her as quickly if touching her flesh had burned him—another unhusbandlike gesture.

''I think whoever killed Jackson thought he killed you at the mine, too.''

"And when he discovered differently, he came back to finish the job?"

"Maybe."

She suspected he'd deliberately softened his opinion so she wouldn't freak, exhibiting a kindness she hadn't suspected. But she was tough, a cop. She wouldn't fall apart. Her legs were only shaking because they'd slid a gazillion feet and had almost gone over a cliff.

Yeah, right. And Alaskan bears were tame.

With their dark clothing against the white snow, they would make easy targets. She suddenly felt vulnerable on the mountainside. Where was the weapon she never let out of her sight?

She glanced over her shoulder and scanned the cliff above but saw no sign of movement in the evergreen trees. "We should take cover."

Sean led her back toward the trail, staying clear of the dangerous areas and taking her onto a well-worn dirt path that curved gently across the terrain. "It's possible someone was hunting deer or elk. Or just watching us through their scope and had no intention of firing."

She shook her head, discounting the possibility. "*You* didn't think so at the time or you wouldn't have hurled us off the mountain." She hurried after him, noticing he hadn't let the gap between them get as big as before. "How many people in town have guns with laser sights?"

"You might as well ask how many people live in town. Everyone has guns. Or easy access to a weapon."

She dusted the snow off her shoulders, wincing at

a sore spot. "I'm focusing my suspicions on Roger, Tyler and Marvin. They are the only ones I'm aware of who know I'm alive and where we're heading. Did they have enough time to reach town and circle back?"

"Tyler, and maybe Roger, could move that quickly. Marv is more comfortable at a poker table than in the woods."

So the brother and Tyler were her prime suspects—not that she was crossing Marvin off her list. "The first thing I need to do is—"

"Rest. I want the doctor to look at that knot on your head."

"I'm fine," she protested, briefly wondering if doctors here made house calls. "But the longer I wait to question the suspects, the easier it'll be for them to forget details or make up lies."

"Maybe so. But I'm not traveling in the dark. So unless you plan to head into town alone…"

"WHERE'S THE PHONE?" Carlie asked before she'd even removed her Arctic parka.

No admiration for the cozy touches nearly foreign in the male-dominated Kesky. No appreciative comments over the homestead he'd worked an entire summer to build. He supposed he shouldn't expect a woman to understand that while he'd cut western red cedar, notched logs and sanded the pine flooring, the mountain cabin had become as much a part of him as this glacier-fed wilderness paradise. His small diesel generator hummed, supplying all the electricity they needed. She had to point out the one convenience he couldn't supply.

"I don't have a phone."

"What?" Her eyes widened, and unwilling to take his word, she stalked across the pine floor, ducked her head into the kitchen, paused, then marched into the bedroom to check for herself.

He shrugged out of his coat and hung it on the hook on the back of the door. He hung up her coat, too. Alaska was no place for a woman. The harsh winters didn't agree with them. Sure, a few tough gals lived in Kesky, but there could be no denying that the long winters took their toll.

A memory of his mother, sick and shoveling snow, made him remember his promise to himself. He'd never ask a woman to stay with him. Especially not a woman accustomed to beaches and tropical heat.

And now he'd gone and done just that. He'd lied to Carlie, telling her they were man and wife. At the time, his lie had seemed the right thing to do. But now...

He considered telling her the truth.

She cleared her throat loudly. "You expect me to stay here without a phone?"

So much for telling the truth. She was already looking for excuses to leave and he'd be damned if he'd give her another one. He walked to the freezer, took out some ice, wrapped it in a towel and handed it to her. "Put this on that lump on your head and maybe the swelling will go down."

"Thanks."

She'd leave in a heartbeat if he didn't give her a powerful reason to stay. Still, he hesitated. Jackson had brought him up better than to become a liar.

Keeping his back to her, he lit a fire in the hearth,

taking a moment to think without her innocent eyes stabbing at him. The lie that they were married wouldn't do her any harm. And if he kept her close, he could keep her safe.

"When we married," he kept his tone soft, non-threatening, "you agreed to live with me." One lie would lead to others. He'd known that and had worked out a plausible explanation on their way down the mountain. Hoping he could keep his story straight, he stood and walked over to her.

With the towel pressed to her head, she tilted up her face and regarded him with fearless curiosity. "Exactly when did we marry?"

"Two weeks ago in Fairbanks. This is your first trip to Kesky and to my cabin. Our cabin," he corrected himself.

"I agreed to live here without ever visiting?" She threw her arms wide, taking in the cabin, the mountain and Kesky.

"Yes." He figured the simpler he kept the story, the better chance he had of making it stick. "How about some supper?"

He walked into the kitchen and she followed him. "I'd like to see a copy of our marriage license."

He opened the fridge, took out pork chops and frozen vegetables. "Hasn't come back from the county courthouse yet."

He could see her mind working. Tomorrow, she'd prance into town, call Fairbanks and learn there hadn't been any marriage. The woman was smart. Determined. He liked that in a woman, even if it did frustrate him.

"Tell me about our wedding," she demanded.

He shrugged. "What do you want to know?"

"Did we have a big party?"

She wanted to know who'd attended. He opened a cabinet and found two potatoes. "It was just you and me at the courthouse. The judge's clerk and secretary were witnesses."

She frowned. "My family—"

"It was too expensive for them to fly at the last minute."

"Last minute?"

He'd decided during the walk down the mountain that the less time he could claim he knew her before they'd married, the less chance there would be of her tripping him up. "We've been exchanging letters for a month, but we'd only met that day."

"What!" Her voice came out a high squeak. "Don't you need a few days for a marriage license, blood tests—"

"I pulled a few strings. You wanted to get married before we—"

"Before we what?" she prodded, hanging on to his every word. He'd always been a good storyteller, learned the skill from his mother. Before she'd died, she'd been too weak to work, but while he'd done the chores, she'd spun fanciful stories for him.

He hesitated as if deliberating whether to answer, then gave it to her with a straight face. "You wanted to get married before we made love."

She slumped into the kitchen chair, eyeing him with a mixture of distrust and horror and just a spark of interest. "How long have we known each other?"

He turned on the stove, set a frying pan on the

burner. "Well, let's see. We married on October 15, so it's been about two weeks."

"No, I mean how long did we know each other *before* we decided to marry?"

"Not counting the letters? A couple of hours."

Her face paled. "A couple of hours?"

"You insisted. You can be very insistent." He grinned. "The way you were kissing me that night, you found me very attractive."

"I must have been out of my mind."

"You were tipsy," he agreed.

She set the towel with the ice down on the table. "I don't drink alcohol."

He tossed the ice into the sink. "Then that explains it."

"Explains what?"

"Why you passed out on me."

"Can I see the letters I wrote you?"

"Didn't save them. Why should I?"

Clearly she wanted to ask him if they'd ever made love. But she didn't. Although he wondered what it would be like to release all her passion in bed, have those sleek arms wrapped around his neck, those long legs around his waist, he should have known she always came back to her investigation.

"So what have I been doing for the past two weeks?"

"I don't know. The morning after our wedding, I flew back on business. You promised to meet me in Kesky. I was beginning to think you weren't going to show up."

"Did I mention that someone was trying to kill me?"

"You remember?" he asked, knowing full well she didn't or she wouldn't be buying his story.

"I'm guessing. But, if I thought someone was after me and I needed to hide out, this seems like the perfect place to do it."

"Maybe not so perfect."

"Yeah, they found me, anyway."

"So you were just using me?" He tried to sound hurt, praying he didn't lay it on too thick. If giving her a guilty conscience would make her stay here with him where he could protect her, he would do so. He recalled his friend's handsome face, his laughing eyes, his open smile. Bill would have wanted Sean to protect her, and the thought helped him act with conviction. "You married me just so I could keep you safe? Are you saying you used me? You didn't mean what you said?"

She rested her elbow on the table, chin in one palm. "I don't remember anything. What did I say?"

"It's not important anymore. You obviously don't have feelings for me. Or maybe you just don't remember them." He paused, baiting her, letting her believe she'd hurt him, used him. He let a note of pleading enter his tone. "You married me. Won't you give us some time to get to know each other?"

He thought she would soften, at least agree to give him a few days. The women in his past would have gone for his line. But she was different from other women. She thought like a cop.

She shook her head. "Staying here could put you in danger."

She was worried about putting him in danger. He almost laughed aloud. Women were not often afraid for him. His size and temperament told them he was well able to take care of himself. The few women who had dated him expected him to take care of them—none that he could recall had ever worried about his safety.

Even without her memory. Carlie was more woman than anyone he'd ever known. Her strength appealed to him on a level he wanted to explore. But first he had to convince her to stay. If she wouldn't remain here for the sake of their marriage, he'd have to use another argument.

He cut the fat off the edges of the pork chops, peppered them and set them in the pan. "I could help you question the men. They don't take kindly to outsiders, and as my wife, they might be more inclined to help you."

"I don't want to put you in danger." Her voice was strong, firm, determined.

He took the seat opposite her and stared directly into her eyes. "Jackson raised me. I owe it to him to find his killer."

She leaned forward and looked him straight in the eye. "And what will you do if it turns out I killed Jackson?"

Chapter Four

Carlie held her breath waiting for his answer.

"If you're guilty, we'll worry about what to do with you later," Sean answered evasively. He walked to the stove and flipped the pork chops, then rinsed the potatoes and placed them and a peeler in front of her. "Right now our first concern has to be keeping you safe."

She began to strip off the potato skins, liking the way he made her feel comfortable in his kitchen by letting her pitch in. The masculine kitchen sported clean lines, the cream countertops bare of all accoutrements. Gleaming copper pots, spatulas and kitchen utensils hung from hooks. But what amazed her were the baskets filled with onions, garlic and herbs.

Obviously Sean liked to cook. For a moment she tried to imagine living here with him, sharing meals. She'd bet the nearest mall was five hundred miles away. She'd have to give up Godiva chocolates and double-fudge-brownie ice cream. But there was something even more wrong with that picture. What would she do all day while he went off to work? She was a cop, accustomed to long hours. Well, no need to fret, she'd be putting in enough hours trying to help solve Jackson's murder.

That thought returned her to her dilemma. "No point in hiding. I'm sure the entire town knows I'm here. How soon until a detective comes knocking on the door?"

He sprinkled the pork chops with garlic powder. "Haskell will have to fly in from Fairbanks. By now, Marvin has probably already sent him a message. But Haskell covers a big territory, and if he's out on another case, it could be a while until he arrives. I'd say we have up to a week before they…"

"Arrest me." She swallowed hard. The circumstantial evidence against her was strong. If she didn't solve this case, she might spend the rest of her life in jail. Thank goodness the law didn't move at the same pace here as it did back home. She'd have to make the most of the time she was free to clear her name. "Tomorrow, I want to talk to Marvin, Tyler and Roger."

Sean stepped close enough for her to smell the clean scent of cedar on him. "How's your head?"

"Sore, but I'm okay." She didn't have time to waste on doctors.

Tilting her head down, he gathered her hair and lifted it off her neck to inspect her injury. His flesh was warm, his skin roughened, his touch gentle, and she recalled how the strength of his hand had stopped her momentum, preventing her from going over the cliff. He'd saved her life.

"You've stopped bleeding, but I still want you to go into Kesky tomorrow. Doc can look at that egg on your head." When she opened her mouth to protest, he held up his hand. "Talking to Roger and Tyler shouldn't be a problem, they work for me. And as for Marvin, he usually hangs out at the local bar— although we'll have to catch him later in the day as he's rarely up before noon."

While he cooked the pork chops, she starting slicing potatoes, and tried not to think how gentle his big hands running through her hair had been. Although she was finally glad to see him exhibit some husbandly tenderness, she didn't like the way her stomach somersaulted when he'd touched her. "I want to go back up to the mine and inspect the murder scene."

His dark eyes turned bleak. "Why?"

"We may have missed something." She spoke quickly before he could disagree. "And I'd like to go through Jackson's house. Did he live alone?"

"Yeah. I have a key." At the mention of Jackson, his expression froze. He placed the pork chops on plates.

She suspected he'd turned away from her to hide his renewed grief over Jackson. Wishing she didn't have to keep bringing up the man's death and hurting him, she said nothing further. They ate dinner in silence, the fire popping comfortably.

After the meal, she started to help clear the dishes, but he sent her to the couch in front of the fire. "Rest."

She didn't argue, grateful not to have to move. The cozy room with its log walls and stone fireplace suited Sean. Rugged like him yet comfortable, the room reflected his personality. Framed photographs of the mountains dotted the walls. A bright black, white, yellow and blue blanket with heavy fringe was folded over the arm of the couch. There was not much furniture; a bookcase and a comfortable leather reading chair that reclined with a good light over it completed the room.

Wind whistled and whined around a corner, drawing her attention to the windows that framed a spectacular silhouette of gray mountains against a black sky. Was it her imagination or was the wind picking up, the snow falling with increasing speed?

Her stomach full and sated, she dozed, and when she opened her eyes, the fire had died down to embers. Sean must have covered her with the blanket, and a quick look into the kitchen revealed it was again immaculate.

Sean was standing over her. "I've changed the sheets. The bedroom is all yours. I'll sleep on the couch."

His words brought her instantly wide awake. With all the difficulties she'd had that day, she hadn't thought ahead to the sleeping arrangements. Kicking the man out of his own bed seemed a poor way to return the hospitality he'd shown her. At six foot four or five, Sean was too large to sleep on the couch. Although she was five nine, she already had a crick in her neck from sleeping half-scrunched.

The king-size bed was big enough to hold them both. She saw no reason for either of them to spend an uncomfortable night. They'd both need to be sharp tomorrow.

While the practical side of her thought out the sleeping arrangements, the wistful side of her wondered how it would feel if he wrapped his arms around her. Right now, she wouldn't object to a little comfort from her husband.

She sat up and slipped her hand into his. "We'll both sleep in the bedroom."

His eyes went wide with shock. "But you don't remember me."

She cocked her head to one side, examining his unnerved reaction. Did he think her a freak due to her loss of memory? Or did he fear sleeping with a murderer? Or was he simply being kind?

She stood and took a step toward him. "I won't put you out of your bed."

He didn't retreat but she sensed he wanted to. "I'll be fine right here."

He didn't look fine. His mouth looked vulnerable, his compelling eyes uneasy as hell. His adoptive father had died and he needed his wife to give him comfort. But he wouldn't admit it. She refused to believe he wanted her to leave him alone. Although he seemed a lone wolf, fit and capable of taking care of himself, she wanted to help ease his grief.

She risked another step forward, giving him a wry glance. "Even if I can't remember our wedding vows, we are husband and wife."

"You don't have to remind me."

On the contrary, he needed lots of reminding. She didn't think he'd take kindly to her belief that he needed a hug, so she appealed to his protective instincts. "Maybe if you just hold me, it'll help my memories return. I read once that scent is one of the most powerful senses."

He whirled away from her and paced like a caged

predator, moving too quickly for her to approach. "Let me get this straight. You want to share a bed tonight…so you can smell me?"

A flush stained her cheeks. Why was he so uncomfortable? She wasn't asking him to make love to her. She only thought to share the bed. But he was acting as if she wanted him to sleep on hot coals.

Full of resolve, she moved quickly, launching herself into his path. He bumped into her, swore, but placed his hands on her shoulders to steady her.

"I don't bite," she teased him. "Not hard, anyway."

He dropped his arms to his sides. Firelight gleamed off the hard planes and angles of his face. "This isn't going to work."

Undeterred, she gave him her most engaging smile. "What isn't?"

"Do you think you can just hustle me into bed and I'll forget all about Jackson? What kind of man—"

"All I wanted was a hug." She spoke quietly, her voice breaking, unable to keep her sadness in check. "But I suppose that's too much comfort to give your wife—especially if she's a murderer."

She hated how needy her voice sounded, but she didn't wait for his response. She'd be damned if she'd allow herself to beg for crumbs of affection. And if he wanted to spend the night alone with his loss—so be it. Whirling on her heel, she marched into the bedroom, wondering what had happened to her luggage. She borrowed a flannel shirt from his drawer to sleep in and headed into the bathroom to change.

Damn him!

She braced her hands on the sink and stared into the mirror. Her face looked just as she remembered it. Round green eyes that tilted up slightly at the edges. A straight nose—regal, her dad called it—and a full mouth. She wished he was here now to wrap his arms around her and give her the hug she wanted so badly.

Her childhood had been a happy one with physical affection dispensed freely between her parents and sister, Kelly. She missed them. Tomorrow, she would go into town and phone home.

Carlie removed her shirt and began to take off her slacks. Something caught the material around her ankle. She looked down.

Her backup gun! Happily, she checked out the weapon holstered at her ankle. A crack shot who religiously practiced her marksmanship on the police firing range, she could protect herself now. With a wide smile, she made sure she'd locked the door behind her. Holding her weapon once again made it easier to strip and turn on the shower.

Hot water soothed her frazzled nerves. A half hour later, she stepped out of the bathroom into the dark bedroom. Dressed in Sean's shirt buttoned to the neck and her panties, she spied Sean fully clothed, lying atop the comforter on the far side of the bed with his hands clasped behind his head. He didn't look at her but stared up at the ceiling.

She flicked off the light. Uneasy, she chattered. "Hope you don't mind, I found a new toothbrush in the medicine cabinet and—"

"Anything I have is yours." His words sounded stilted, but she appreciated the thought.

She slipped the gun under her side of the mattress. "Thanks. I'll pick up a few things tomorrow when I go—"

"When *we* go. I don't want you out of my sight."

So he'd come into the bedroom to check up on her. He thought she would run away and he wanted to be sure she stayed in town until Haskell arrived to arrest her.

Ignoring her anger, ignoring him, she flipped up the covers and climbed into bed. Deliberately, she turned on her side and did her best to pretend he didn't exist.

His voice, husky and measured in the dark, blanketed her with warmth. "I'm not sure we'll be hiking into Kesky tomorrow. Snow may sock us in."

She scrunched her eyes shut hard. "Great. Now the weather is conspiring against me."

"There is an up side," he spoke soothingly, when it should be her soothing him after his loss.

"And that is?" she prodded.

"No planes will fly in or out in this weather."

Haskell, the homicide detective, would have to fly in from Fairbanks. Maybe the weather would buy her an extra day or two of freedom.

Carlie held still, intensely aware of the man in the bed next to her. She didn't fall asleep for a very long time.

SEAN ALREADY HAD bacon and eggs frying and coffee brewing before Carlie exited the bedroom. She looked wonderful with her blond hair swinging freely over her shoulders, her eyes sparkling pine green. "'Morning, sleepyhead. How's your head?''

"Much better, thanks." Before she could say another word, the roar of an engine interrupted her train of thought.

"Snowmobile," Sean explained. "It's how most of us go visiting during the winter."

The engine died. Someone banged at the door.

Carlie paled.

Sean turned down the stove. "Relax. Haskell can't be here yet. This isn't flying weather. The winds are gusting at forty-five knots. But it didn't snow enough to sock us in."

Sean opened the door and gestured his visitors inside along with a blast of cold air and several drifting snowflakes. Ian Finley, Kesky's wealthiest citizen, took off his ski mask and scarf, stomping the snow off his bunny boots, oversize white insulated rubber boots that kept one's feet from freezing and making them appear twice normal size. Beside him, Roger removed orange outerwear, and then both finally peeled out of their Arctic parkas.

Ian was the kind of man who usually stayed in town behind his desk at the bank. And Sean couldn't recall the last time Roger had paid him a visit.

Sean's curiosity rose to the surface. "You boys are up early. How about some coffee?"

"Sounds good," Roger muttered, his eyes red-rimmed from either whiskey or tears. Jackson's brother was taking the old prospector's death hard.

Roger scowled at Carlie but spoke to Sean. "She get her memory back yet?"

Sean glanced at her and she shook her head. He

was glad to see a little color return to her face as he hastily made introductions. ''Ian, meet my wife, Carlie. Carlie, this is Ian Finley. He owns the bank, the general store and does some lawyering on the side.''

Ian removed his hat, revealing his bald head. Rich and successful, Ian dressed the part. Wearing a crisp white shirt, dark suit jacket, slacks and a tie, he looked ready for business on Wall Street.

Must be important for him to have ridden out here in this weather. Ian preferred others come to him. He liked sitting behind his fancy desk at the bank, lording it over all the people who asked for a loan. His daddy had been a banker, and his daddy before him. He probably knew down to the penny the net worth of every citizen of Kesky.

Ian looked through his gold wire-rimmed glasses from Carlie to Sean. ''Heard you got hitched.'' Ian stared at Carlie, his face gleaming with interest. ''Heard you also lost your memory. Whole town's talking about the murder. Didn't know whether or not to believe the story.'' He clucked his tongue. ''Lots of strange goings-on around our small town.''

Sean poured the men coffee. After they seated themselves around the kitchen table, Carlie handed them each a mug and spoke carefully. ''You think marriage is odd?''

''No, ma'am,'' Ian said. ''I'm a married man myself.''

From the gleam in Carlie's eyes, Sean suspected she was up to something. Carlie poured three packets of sugar into her coffee. ''You didn't think Sean would ever marry?''

So she wanted information about him. Did she suspect the story he'd told her wasn't true?

Ian's glasses started to fog. He took them off and wiped them. "Well, Sean sure kept you a secret. But I was referring to Jackson's murder." He plunked his freshly wiped glasses on his distinguished nose. "I'm sorry, Sean. Jackson was a good man, a hard worker, honest."

Roger refused to look at Carlie. He tapped Ian on the elbow. "Enough jawing. Get to it."

Sean put on more eggs and extra slices of bacon. "Get to what?"

Roger frowned. "The reading of my brother's will."

"Yes, well as I already told you, there're a few complications."

Roger glared at Sean and jerked his thumb at Ian. "He wouldn't explain nothing until you could hear him, too."

Carlie shoved back her chair. "Excuse me, gentlemen. This doesn't concern—"

"If you're his wife, it does." Ian pulled a packet of papers from his suit pocket. At Sean's puzzled expression, he explained. "Jackson left his will with me. Do you want the long legalese version or the short?"

Sean scooped up the bacon and drained the strips on paper towels. Deftly, he placed the eggs on plates, noting Carlie had already set extra places at the table. Jackson had never mentioned his will, and Sean had never asked. He was more than content with his forty-five-percent share in the mine.

Roger ignored the food Carlie placed on the table. "Just get to it."

"Fine. Fine." Ian swallowed a bite of bacon and cleared his throat. "Jackson left his land and his cabin and the contents to his brother, Roger."

Roger shot a look of triumph at Sean. "What about the Dog Mush?" Roger prodded.

"I'm getting to the mine. Let me do this in an orderly fashion."

"More coffee?" Carlie asked brightly, her sunny smile a futile attempt to cut the tension.

While Sean appreciated her effort, he didn't understand Roger's animosity toward him. He'd loved Jackson and had nothing to gain from the man's death. Roger had been there when Jackson took Sean into his home. He had to know how much Sean had loved his brother. And even taking into account Roger's hot temper, his considering Sean could be responsible for the beloved old man's murder sickened him.

For a moment he understood how Carlie must have felt to have her husband accuse her of murder. And in truth, he couldn't picture Bill lying to his wife with the duplicity Sean had. At least Sean had the consolation of knowing he was innocent. Carlie didn't know what had happened. With her memory gone, she could only wonder if somehow she had committed an atrocious crime.

And despite what must have been a troubled night, here she was trying to ease the tension in the room while her own plans to investigate the murder and clear herself had been put on hold. His estimation of her rose another notch.

But he kept his face a mask, unwilling to allow even a hint of his feelings about Carlie to show. Jackson had taught him that patience and listening often won over a man far more than hot words, and Sean sorely missed him. He consoled himself with memories he'd keep close to his heart for the rest of his days.

Ian shuffled through pages of documents. Roger shifted restlessly, combing his fingers through his beard. Carlie shot Sean a look of sympathy.

"What's the problem?" Roger asked.

"Jackson's affairs are complicated. I need to say this—"

Roger slapped a palm on the table. "Just tell us who he left the mine to."

Carlie reached out and squeezed Sean's hand as if she thought he needed support. Her hand was warm, soft, and he almost squeezed affectionately before he remembered his lie and snatched it away. Almost as if expecting his move, she allowed a wry quirk of her lips.

"Okay. Here's the situation. Thirty years ago, Jackson staked a claim to the mine."

"So?" Roger interrupted. "That's old news. Get to the point, already."

"Bear with me. I want the ownership progression to be straight in all of our minds. Fifteen years ago, he gave a forty-five-percent share to Sean McCabe."

"We know that—"

"And over the intervening years, he either sold or gave two-percent shares to five other minor investors. So at the time of his death, Jackson still owned a forty-five-percent share."

Roger glared at Carlie, Sean and Ian. "And who did he leave it to?"

"To Sean McCabe."

Roger stood so fast, he knocked over his chair. "And Sean's new wifey murdered my brother. Ain't that just tidy?"

Carlie gasped.

Sean kept his voice cool, his eyes steady on Roger. "I resent your implication."

"And I resent that your wife murdered my brother so you could inherit his share of the mine."

Ian raised both hands into the air. "Hold on, folks. I'm not done."

"I've heard all I need to," Roger muttered.

"You can wait inside or not, as you like. But Sean won't be any richer tomorrow than he is today unless the Dog Mush hits the mother lode."

Deciding Roger was no immediate threat to Carlie, Sean turned his attention to Ian. "I don't understand."

"Jackson mortgaged his share of the mine." Ian paused and wiped his glasses. "I'm afraid he didn't even pay the interest on the loan. Now, if you can raise the cash to cover his debt, his share of the mine is yours. If not, I'm afraid my bank is your new partner."

A loan. Now Sean knew how the old man had paid for his four expensive years at Harvard. While Jackson was the most generous of men, he'd always been secretive about his financial affairs. He'd mortgaged the mine and never said a word. Sean's throat closed tight; he owed Jackson so much.

Roger frowned at Sean in suspicion. "You didn't know about the mortgage, did you?"

"I don't appreciate your filthy insinuations. Get out of my home." Sean's voice was still low, but he was half hoping Roger would resist so he could throw the man out.

Carlie put a tentative hand on Sean's arm. At the same time she spoke firmly to Roger. "I think you should leave now."

Roger backed away, his eyes angry. "My brother took you in when your own folks didn't want you. I told Jackson you would come to no good. But he was so proud to send you to that fancy college back east." Roger cackled. "But you weren't satisfied with what he gave you out of the generosity of his heart. You had to have more. But there wasn't any more."

Sean stood slowly. "Get out."

"Or what, you'll have her kill me, too?"

Carlie shook her head. "I didn't—"

"You killed my brother for nothing. You won't see one penny of profit from that mine. And your wife, she's going to jail. You won't get away with murder. I'll see to it."

Sean's ears roared with the pounding of his heart. He'd love nothing better than to place his fist into Roger's mouth and stop his horrific accusations. But Carlie's hand on his forearm made him think twice.

His first obligation was to find Jackson's murderer. He barely listened to Ian.

The banker shoved papers into his briefcase. "I don't know a thing about mining. You've been running the Dog Mush long enough to keep her profitable. And come spring, when you reopen the mine, I won't be making any changes in the foreseeable future. Why don't we get together next week and you can fill me in on—''

''We'll do that.''

The men left in a blast of engine noise and Sean watched them go, his mind hardening with resolve after the ugly scene. Carlie dumped uneaten food into the trash and cleaned the kitchen but didn't say a word. He appreciated a woman who knew when to be silent.

Until now, until he'd become so personally involved, Sean hadn't realized how ugly suspicion could become. Were all of Roger's and Jackson's friends going to be suspicious of him and Carlie? He watched her in the kitchen, wiping the counter of crumbs, her eyes worried.

Right about now, he could use that hug she'd offered so freely last night. He'd been a fool to turn her away. But she was Bill's widow—not Sean's wife. And he wouldn't take advantage of her affection.

When he once again had his thoughts under control, he turned to her. ''Do you want to go into Kesky and see the doctor?''

''The ice did the trick and the swelling's down. I'd rather do some investigating.''

''You're the boss. Where do we start?''

Chapter Five

Carlie stared out the window at the snow. The skies were partly sunny, but fog had settled into every pocket and cranny. Yesterday she'd thought the mountain peaks spectacular, yet today she shivered at the prospect of hiking over steep, snow-covered trails.

She turned from the window. Sean stalked toward the front door, gliding as quietly and smoothly as a shadow, reminding her how much he seemed a part of these untamable mountains.

She glanced at a map on the wall, then back at Sean. "How far from here is Jackson's cabin?"

Sean opened a closet and disappeared inside. "Not far. Maybe ten miles."

"Ten miles?" That meant a round-trip distance of twenty miles. While a man like Sean would consider the hike just a morning jaunt, she didn't look forward to the prospect. "I don't suppose you have a car?"

"Sure do." Sean's muffled voice came from deep in the closet. The clang of metal, falling boxes and rustling clothing mingled with his husky reply. "My car's garaged in town. It's already been stored for winter. I won't break her out until spring.''

Not for the first time, Carlie wondered how she could have agreed to live here. No phones. No cars. No neighbors within sight. Just snow and forests and mountain men who didn't seem to get lonely. The one she'd married apparently didn't even have a need for hugs.

''Got it.'' Sean emerged from the closet with an adorable smudge of dirt on his squared chin and a bundle of rubberlike clothing in his hands.

She hurried over to help him. ''What is this?''

''Snowsuits.''

What was wrong with the clothing they'd worn yesterday? ''For the snow?''

His gray eyes twinkled. ''For the snowmobile. Unless you want to walk?''

Heat rose to Carlie's cheeks. He'd told her everyone up here traveled by snowmobile, and she should have recognized the black rubbery outfits were similar to the orange ones Ian and Roger had worn. She thought about Florida's balmy weather where her biggest clothing decision was whether or not to carry a jacket outside. Dressing correctly in Alaska wasn't a mere fashion statement. Her choice of apparel might make the difference between freezing and survival.

By the time she'd donned her Arctic parka, a woolen scarf and the snowmobile suit, she felt thirty pounds overweight, sweaty and eager to go outside. ''You sure we aren't dressed too warmly?''

Sean closed the door behind them and didn't bother with a lock. He led her behind his cabin to a shed she hadn't noticed yesterday. "Any speed over twenty miles an hour, the wind chill factor is considerable."

Dressed in black from knitted hat to thick boots, he looked fit for this rugged land. Moving with the ease of a wolf on a lazy morning, he opened the shed and gestured her inside.

"Haven't ridden her since last winter, so I need to check a few things."

She thought he was referring to the motor or gasoline, mechanical stuff. He surprised her when instead of opening the engine compartment he lifted the seat.

Although Sean expected the drive to take no more than half an hour, she saw him pack the snowmobile with care. Inside the storage compartment beneath the seat, Carlie saw emergency flares, a map encased in plastic, a pot, a knife, matches and a lighter, a mirror, a first aid kit, a tightly rolled sleeping bag and rope.

She pointed to several shrink-wrapped packages. "What's that?"

He handed her a helmet. "Dehydrated food. It lasts for years and can come in handy in an emergency."

He sounded so casual, like someone packing chewing gum to take on a plane ride. She didn't know whether to be glad they were prepared or to worry over dangers she hadn't the knowledge to cope with. With determination, she put the thought of ending up stranded in these mountains behind her. Sean obviously knew what he was doing.

He started the engine and eased out of the shed.

She closed the door and hopped on behind him. The wide padded seat was surprisingly comfortable.

''Hang on,'' he told her, with a hint of eagerness in his tone.

She placed her hands around his waist, held tight, thinking they would jerk forward. But he increased speed slowly, letting her get the feel of the snowmobile. The smooth riding machine took the occasional bump with a minimum of jarring. Wind whipped her suit and she was grateful for the warmth of her protective clothing, appreciative of Sean's wide chest and shoulders that broke the wind.

Sean circled the cabin as if marking his territory before heading back toward the steep trail they'd slid down yesterday. Recalling their near death at the cliff's edge, she shuddered. Tumbling off the mountain at thirty miles an hour—

Perhaps she should have insisted on walking. She squared her shoulders.

Stop it. Don't you have enough trouble?

Carlie took a deep breath and brushed all thoughts of danger aside. Sean handled the vehicle with the same dexterity as she handled her weapon. He knew the mountain. He kept the pace appropriate to the terrain. Where the trail narrowed and curved into sharp S's, he slowed.

For the first time since she'd awakened without her memory, she relaxed and took in the beauty around her. The rising sun burned off pockets of fog. Eagles soared overhead. Peace settled over her as they sped past a trickling waterfall and scared off a deer drinking at a rock pool.

The majesty of the land had a certain soothing

effect. Besides the snowmobile, she couldn't see any signs that mankind inhabited the planet. No airplanes overhead. No honking horns from traffic. No telephone lines spoiled Mother Nature. And each breath of air was as sweet and fresh as mountain pine.

All too soon, the ride ended in front of a cabin similar in design to Sean's, although the logs appeared older, as did the shingles curling through the layer of snow that had managed to stick to the steep A-frame roof. The stone chimney didn't puff even a smidgen of smoke, lending a deserted air to the site. Snow around the cabin appeared pristine and untouched except by squirrel and raven tracks.

Sean shut off the engine and helped her with her helmet. "What exactly are we looking for?"

"Jackson's personal papers. A diary." She unzipped her oversuit, her body warming in the midday sun. "Phone bills."

"He didn't have a phone." Sean reached into his pocket and took out a set of keys, but the front door was unlocked.

Carlie surmised security in the mountains wasn't a problem.

She strode inside, noting a handheld radio amid the dust and clutter. "What about cell phones?"

"When the peaks aren't blocking a direct satellite link, the minerals in the mountains play havoc with the signals. We mostly use radio and walkie-talkies."

While he spoke in the husky voice she was beginning to rely on, she looked around the cabin and peeled off the protective layers of clothing. Outside an electric generator squatted against the southern wall, and as backup, inside, a potbellied stove dominated the den next to a huge stack of split firewood. A dilapidated leather sofa sat next to a late-model big-screen TV.

Noticing the direction of her gaze, Sean's lips curved upward. "During the winter Jackson holed up here with videos of almost every movie made. He had quite a collection."

Glad to be free of the outer bulky clothing, she kept her parka on to avoid the chill. Jackson's home wasn't equipped with central heat. "Are his videos valuable?"

"I doubt it. Why?"

"I'm looking for a motive to commit murder. Money is often right up there as a reason. And money usually leaves a trail of paperwork."

Sean threaded a hand through his dark hair. "Every nickel Jackson had he plowed back into the mine." He led the way through the kitchen-living area into a back office. "This is where he kept his papers."

A calendar hung on the wall along with black-and-white pictures of miners. When Sean moved out of the way and Carlie saw the stacks of papers overflowing the desk and spilling onto the floor, the file cabinets with open drawers too full to close, she groaned. "Didn't he ever throw anything away?"

Sean strode forward and cleaned papers off two chairs. "Maybe we'll find some clues in this mess."

"Too bad we don't have ten years."

He blew the dust off the chair and gestured to her to have a seat. "Looks worse than it is. I used to help him keep his papers straight when I lived here."

She cleared a pile of file folders from her feet. "When was that?"

"Before I left for college."

"You don't look that old," she teased. When he didn't respond with a smile, she wondered if she should be so flippant. Jackson had obviously been like a father to him. And this was the first time Sean had been back since the old prospector's death. The cabin must hold many good memories for him and she felt as if she was intruding.

She rested one boot on her chair and bit her lip. "Look, I'm sorry. I didn't mean to be disrespectful of your feelings. Coming back here must be difficult for you."

"Thanks for the sentiment." He stood stiffly, spoke stiffly, his features a mask. "But having you with me is... You keep distracting me from..."

He looked as if he needed another hug. But she wasn't ready to renew that particular conversation. Instead she reached up and smoothed away the smudge he'd gotten on his chin when he'd retrieved the snowmobile suits from the closet.

His jaw was firm, his freshly shaven skin warm. She was close enough to smell his soap mixing with a clean male scent that reminded her of wintergreen. All of a sudden the room seemed crowded.

Sean stared into her eyes, then took her hand away from his face. "I'll tackle the desk. Why don't you try the filing cabinet?"

Fine. If he wanted to reject her every effort to comfort him—so be it. She'd done her wifely duty. Only she didn't feel like a wife. He wouldn't let her.

Turning away before he could read the hurt in her

eyes, she stared at the files. "What's the name of Jackson's bank?"

"Kesky National."

Her eyebrows rose.

"Ian's granddaddy had big dreams. As far as I know, the family never even opened a second branch."

"But you told me Ian is rich. And if Kesky isn't that big, where did the family make their money?"

"Ian's granddaddy mined gold right alongside Jackson's father. He struck a thick vein, sold out and opened the bank and the store. Buying the land around the railroad made him even wealthier."

While she found the small-town history interesting, she'd best dig into the files. "Did Jackson file in alphabetical order?"

"Yep. Try under the *B*s."

"*B* for Kesky?"

"*B* for bank."

"I suppose I'll find his legal papers under *L?*"

Sean nodded. "Now you've got his secret filing system down pat."

Two hours later, Carlie had uncovered the deed to the cabin and another to the mine. Her nose itched from dust mites and she longed for a shower. She'd sorted and stacked hundreds of assayer's slips documenting the sale of gold dust and gold nuggets. But she never found any canceled checks.

She stretched her shoulders and sighed. "Where could Jackson have kept his bank statements?"

Sean looked up from where he sat behind the roll-top desk. "I doubt he had any."

"What?" She looked up wearily and rubbed the

crick in her neck. No one could run a business without a bank account.

"Jackson paid our suppliers in gold. He paid his bill at the general store in gold. Even paid for Sally—"

"Sally?"

Sean hesitated, as if debating how much to tell her. Although she didn't know him well, she discerned her question made him uncomfortable and that made her all the more curious.

Finally, he answered. "Sally is Jackson's lady friend."

"Lady friend?"

"They had an arrangement. She gave him comfort and he helped her—"

"He paid her for comfort?"

Sean winced. "She lived in town and he paid her bills. And he lived up here alone."

Carlie frowned. "Does Sally have arrangements with any other men?"

"Not lately." Sean's eyes lightened and his tone teased. "Why? Are you afraid I might visit Sally?"

"Not exactly." Her thoughts wrapped around the murder investigation, trying to grasp the situation.

"Sally's gorgeous—" Sean winked at Carlie, his comment coming from left field "—but I'm strictly a one-woman man."

She hadn't seen this lighter side of Sean before and rather liked it. While she hated to bring the conversation back to murder when he was trying so hard to lighten the mood, she didn't have time for playfulness. "Maybe Jackson was killed over this woman."

Sean's eyes darkened. "That hadn't occurred to me."

"She could have been two-timing him." Carlie bit her lower lip. "Or maybe someone wanted Jackson out of the picture so they could move in on his woman. Or maybe Jackson and Sally had a lover's quarrel and she—"

"Hush." He held up his hand, and pointed to his ear, indicating she should listen.

What had he heard?

Carlie listened hard, barely breathing. Was someone out there eavesdropping on their conversation?

In the den, out of her line of sight, someone cocked a shotgun.

Automatically, Carlie checked for a second exit and reached for the gun she wore strapped to her ankle, the gun Sean knew nothing about. Reluctant to display her ace in the hole, she nevertheless couldn't allow someone to fire on them without fighting back. While she might escape and squeeze through the back window, Sean's shoulders wouldn't make it.

"Come out with your hands up," a gruff voice ordered.

Sean raised his hands above his shoulders and boldly stepped through the door. "Roger, is that you? It's Sean. I'm coming out."

No!

How could he offer himself as a target? And to Roger, of all people.

Weapon drawn, Carlie darted low, through the doorway, past Sean, and rolled. At the same moment, Roger raised his shotgun.

Rolling into the room, Carlie stabilized on her belly and aimed at Roger.

Sean pounced on top of her, grasping her wrist, knocking the wind from her straining lungs. "Don't fire."

Was he nuts? Didn't Sean understand that Roger was about to shoot them?

Carlie had Roger targeted in her sights. He stood still, not even trying to run. With Sean's hard body pinning her to the floor, his powerful wrist twisting hers, he forced her to drop the weapon.

She'd expected Sean to, at the very least, stay out of her way. His tackling her and protecting Roger made no sense.

"Hold still."

Not in this lifetime. Suspicion and anger gave her strength. "You son of a—"

Roger set down his shotgun and collapsed onto a stool. "Where did she get the gun?"

She drew up her knee, aiming for Sean's groin. Sean twisted, and instead of striking a vital area, her knee glanced off the muscle of his thigh.

Damn. She rammed an elbow into his gut and took satisfaction in his grunt of pain. Overpowered and underleveraged, she couldn't hope to win. But she refused to let him hold her down so Roger could kill her.

"Hey. Calm down. I don't want to hurt you," Sean murmured in her ear.

"Of course not." She would have spit in his eye, but he flipped her to her stomach. "You just want to pin me down so Roger can do it."

Roger opened a metal flask and sipped. "Is she crazy?"

"I'm not certain." Sean eased some of his weight off her, but not enough so that she could threaten him with another blow.

Slowly, she inched her fingers toward her gun. But with Sean's chest pressed to her back, he couldn't help but notice her struggle. With a casual movement, he scooped the gun from the floor and then released her.

She scrambled to her feet, her chest heaving to draw oxygen into her lungs. What the hell was going on? This morning Sean had thrown Roger out of his house. Just now, Roger had aimed the gun and...and...

Sean simply rolled to his side, rested his head in his palm and eyed her warily. "You aren't going to hurt me again, are you?"

Hurt him? She might as well have pounded granite. Pummeling him with all her strength hadn't caused a lick of damage.

"I..." She looked from Roger, who sat on the stool sipping whiskey, to Sean lying sprawled on the floor. Neither man looked particularly threatening. This morning they'd acted like mortal enemies. Now they were both eyeing her as if she were from Pluto.

She pointed a finger at Jackson's brother. "You had your gun aimed at Sean." Or maybe Roger had tried to shoot her. The entire situation was confusing.

Sean shrugged. "If Roger had wanted me dead, my heart wouldn't still be beating."

Carlie eyed Roger. Jackson's brother raised his flask to Sean in a toast. "That's the truth." He sipped, closed the flask and flipped it to Sean, who caught it with one hand.

This sudden lack of animosity between them confused her. ''But you had the gun pointed—''

''Didn't know who I would find in my brother's cabin. I recognized Sean's snowmobile but it could have been stolen. Didn't mean no harm.''

Carlie rubbed her temple. ''You always walk in with a loaded gun?''

Roger rolled his eyes at the ceiling. ''This is my house now. You heard Ian read the will. If Sean wanted to come snooping, he should have asked for an invite.''

Carlie didn't get it. Yesterday, Sean and Roger had argued. This morning Roger had practically accused Sean of murdering Jackson, and now they were both acting as if it were nothing unusual for Roger to aim a gun at Sean. And they had the nerve to question her sanity?

She wished she was back in Florida dealing with the good-old-boy network. At least she understood Southern male chauvinism. But these Alaskan miners were hard to figure out. It must be a mountain-man thing. Like a fistfight that ended in a draw and both men respecting the other's punch enough to make friends.

Realizing she'd misinterpreted the situation made her face flush. How the hell should she have guessed? Obviously, Sean and Roger went way back.

''Find anything in Jackson's papers?'' Roger asked.

Sean took a sip from the flask and passed it back. ''Nope. We haven't finished.''

"*You* can come back any time. Just ask first."

"She didn't kill him, you know," Sean said conversationally.

Roger didn't even look her way. "So then, who killed my brother?"

Sean's tone hardened. "We're going to find out. I promise you."

Carlie leaned against the counter where she could eyeball both men. "Did your brother mention any enemies, any unusual business problems he might have been having?"

"Jackson didn't talk much," Roger told her.

On a hunch, Carlie prodded. "Maybe he talked more to Sally?"

Roger rolled his eyes at the ceiling. "You leave her out of this."

"But she might know something important about your brother, something you and Sean don't know." Carlie pushed harder, thinking Roger a mite overprotective.

Roger picked up his one-barreled shotgun and waved the gun at the ceiling. "You've outstayed your welcome."

"Okay." Carlie didn't want to set off the man's temper. No matter how harmless Sean thought Roger was, she'd prefer to get out while the getting was good. "We're going. Thanks for the hospitality."

Sean rolled to his feet and rubbed his upper lip. Carlie could have sworn he was hiding a grin behind his palm. Maybe if he was the one being accused of murder he wouldn't think the situation was so all-fired funny.

They'd spent a good part of the day here and

learned little. At this rate, her investigation wouldn't end before the snow melted next spring. Rubbing her hip, which ached from her wild tumble across the floor, she preceded Sean out the door, trying to forget how easily he'd overpowered her.

For a moment back there when she'd been fighting with Sean, she'd recalled playfully wrestling with another man, a man with blond hair and laughing blue eyes. Were her memories starting to surface? And if so, who was the mysterious man in her past?

Swollen gray clouds blocked the sun and snow fell heavily from the darkened sky. Carlie shivered, and even her protective clothing couldn't dispel the cold seeping into her bones. The day was almost over, and she wasn't any nearer to clearing her name.

Perhaps once she reached town and a phone, she could resolve the mystery of the two missing years that still eluded her. But no one beside the murderer could tell her who had killed Jackson. And the killer wasn't talking.

She couldn't stop thinking that she didn't belong in this frozen land. A wolf howled in the distance and she stepped closer to Sean. She had a sudden hankering for sun-kissed beaches and gentle breezes whispering through the palm fronds of southern Florida.

Without her having to ask, Sean returned her weapon. His lips curled up in a wry grin. "Try not to shoot any two-legged creatures."

"I'm not making any promises," she replied lightly. But his teasing banter couldn't pull her from gloomy thoughts. Only the familiar weight in her ankle holster and the knowledge she soon would be speaking to her family kept her spirits up.

For ten minutes they rode in silence. She expected Sean to head downward to town at the fork she'd noted on the ride over. But he steered the snowmobile back the way they'd come, ignoring the trail to Kesky.

Shouting over the roar of the engine, she fought to be heard. "I need to go to town. Use the phone. Talk to Sally."

"Not now. Weather's coming in." Sean jerked his thumb at a mountain peak to the north.

Above the entire valley, the sky thickened with tumbling vapors, interspersed with diminishing tracts of blue. Cold whipped down the mountain. Arctic birds called Ptarmigan roosted together, conserving body heat. While minute by minute the belching cloud deck descended, growing thicker, darker, spitting snow at them like bullets.

Could the snowmobile outrun the weather? Sean seemed to think so. But as unappealing as spending more time with Roger would be, Carlie wondered if the wisest course would be to turn around.

"Should we go back?"

"We're more than halfway home."

She'd never call this winter wilderness home. Despite her helmet, wind tunneled behind her face plate and tiny snowflakes stung her cheeks and lips. Pummeling snow found its way into the crevices between glove and sleeve.

Her teeth chattered, seemingly of their own volition, and she could no longer feel her fingertips. Carlie kept reminding herself that this snow would keep the authorities from flying in. The horrible weather would give her more time to investigate—if she didn't freeze to death first.

Surely they must have almost reached Sean's cabin? Sean started a curve uphill and she peeked behind her, over her right shoulder. The darkest clouds chased them with a vengeance. Glancing forward, around Sean's shoulder, she squinted through the snow, searching for his cabin.

She'd give two months of memories for a hot shower and a mug of steaming coffee. But the view ahead looked bleak. Snow, rocks and a straight line that didn't belong.

Oh, God. A line stretched between two spruce trees.

At neck level.

There was no time to stop. No time to warn Sean.

Reacting on pure instinct, Carlie threw her arms around Sean and toppled him sideways off the speeding snowmobile. "Roll. Roll, damn it. Roll."

Once again the two of them tumbled, banging against the snowdrifts, skidding along patches of ice. Luckily the area was flat and they needed only to contend with their momentum from the bike.

Carlie slid to a bruising stop against some gooseberry brush. Dazed, she stumbled to her feet. She couldn't see Sean. Why didn't he stand up where she could find him? He must be hurt.

And she was all alone.

Chapter Six

"Sean!"

Carlie called his name repeatedly. He had to be nearby, but visibility was down to two feet. With the snow falling so thickly, she could barely see her hand in front of her face. In moments, her helmet's visor was filmed with snow. She raised the plastic face plate to see and pelting flakes lashed her cheeks and chin.

Snow coated her eyelashes and she blinked, unwilling to take one step until she got her bearings. Her walking off a cliff in a panicked rush would do neither Sean nor her any good. She had to keep her head. Sean could be hurt.

Squinting, she tried to find the snowmobile with the survival gear Sean had packed. But she couldn't see the turquoise vehicle. Wasn't even sure of which direction to look after her tumble.

With snow in her collar, snow running down her back, she was shivering hard and she supposed she should be grateful that her body still had the capability to fight the cold. Tremors running through her indicated that hypothermia had not set in.

She'd lost a glove in her tumble. She looked down and found it buried in an inch of snow. Gritting her teeth, she forced herself to put the icy glove back on her hand, figuring any protection, even soggy and wet, might save her from frostbite.

When she picked up her glove, she noted the marks in the snow from her tumble. If she could follow her tracks back to the snowmobile, she could circle and see where Sean had gotten lost.

A dozen steps later, she stumbled over him. Kneeling in the snow and ignoring the cold, she looked for a sign he was still alive. "Sean."

When he didn't answer, she rolled him to his back, took off his helmet and leaned over him. Relief filled her when his warm breath hit her cheek. He was alive.

But how badly injured? His swarthy features looked pale, but no blood flowed from his ears, nose or mouth. While all cops had first aid training, she didn't know what to do next. She didn't dare undress him in the cold to check for broken bones or internal injuries. She couldn't exactly call 911 for help. And leaving him on the mountain while she went back to Roger's cabin, that is if she could find Roger's cabin, seemed a foolhardy option.

Deciding her primary objective had to be keeping Sean warm, she debated leaving him to search for the snowmobile and blankets. Suppose she couldn't find him again? With the snowstorm raging around her, her tracks would fill within minutes.

Lifting him under his arms, she used her weight, attempting to drag him. At five foot nine, Carlie wasn't a small woman, yet she couldn't move his bulk more than a few inches.

Dropping to her knees beside him, she lightly slapped his cheek. "Come on. Wake up."

His eyelids fluttered.

"Stay with me, Sean."

He groaned.

"I'm not leaving you here to die. I want to help, but I don't know what to do."

His gun-metal gray eyes opened. "You could try mouth-to-mouth resuscitation."

Obviously he was breathing just fine. She was so happy to hear him speak, she chuckled. "Are you okay?"

"Just a little cold." One snowy eyebrow rose suggestively. "Warm me up."

"How?"

"With a kiss." He uncoiled his arms from under him with a deceptively lazy action that didn't quite camouflage his mischievous gaze. Gently he pulled her down on top of him. His mouth closed over hers. Warmth poured into her. She had no sense of being dragged from the familiar and the safe. She welcomed the new and exciting step of intimacy. She knew she had been kissed before, but never with such intensity, with such overwhelming heat.

If she'd been standing, she would have learned the true meaning of being weak in the knees. Luckily she lay prone, with nowhere to run. But she didn't want to escape, she wanted to stay in his arms, explore the fiery sensations. As far as she was concerned, it had taken him long enough to initiate a kiss.

But he was more than making up for his slow start. She clenched his hair in her hand, sampling a few more degrees of the sexual heat he discharged like lightning bolts. With a bold thoroughness, he shot sizzling fire straight to her toes.

He pulled back from her swollen lips and locked gazes. "Damn. I shouldn't have done that."

"Excuse me?"

"I'm sorry."

Sorry for kissing her? He'd gone from passionate to indifference in the space she drew a breath. Before he could see her eyes fill with tears at this sudden rejection, she rolled away. "Don't you dare apologize for kissing me. Husbands are supposed to kiss their wives."

Sean muttered something unintelligible, brushed off the snow and regained his feet.

First he'd scared her half to death, lying still as a corpse in the snow. Then he'd come alive, surprising her with a passion she'd never expected. And finally he'd rejected her with no explanation. Her hurt blazed into anger. "I like you better flat on your back."

He towered over her, in full mountain-man mode. Flinty-eyed, stone-hearted and steel-jawed. "Is that why you put me there?"

How dare he suggest she'd risked their lives to steal a kiss. She sucked in air. "You have to be the most arrogant, conceited, stubborn man I know. I saved your life."

He crossed his arms over his chest and looked around the clearing. "Well, this arrogant, conceited, stubborn man would like some proof."

"You want proof. Fine." She grabbed his hand and tugged him back toward the snowmobile, following his faint tracks in the snow. "There's your proof." She pointed.

In front of the overturned vehicle, she found what she'd spotted while riding the snowmobile. Someone had strung a wire between two trees, directly across their path. "I assume even your neck isn't rigid enough to withstand that kind of punishment."

He gave her a wry look. "Snowmobiles have brakes."

"There wasn't time to stop." She pointed to the overturned machine, not ten feet from the wire.

"I don't suppose you recall my banking into a turn? Stopping is much easier if one turns the vehicle uphill at the same time one brakes."

A flush of heat rose to her cheeks. He'd seen the wire and had been in the process of turning them away from danger when she'd so precipitously yanked him off the machine. Embarrassment churned in her stomach at her mistake. Her instinctive reactions didn't work in the Alaskan wilderness. She had no business making life-and-death decisions out here on the mountain.

She swallowed her anger. "You could have said something. Warned me."

"You didn't give me time."

She'd seen the wire and acted immediately and now she felt the fool. At least he wasn't hurt. If the machine wasn't damaged, she'd done no real harm.

She expected him to lecture her about being careful, about letting him take charge. After all, he was the expert here. However angry she got with Sean over the lack of intimacy in their marriage, she relished the way he took in stride her need to be a full partner. He didn't coddle. He didn't lecture. And just like when he handed her back her weapon, he seemed ready to let the subject drop, and for that she was thankful.

Another memory of the blond man burst inside her head. A soft grin on his face, he lectured her about her gun, telling her she shouldn't sleep with her weapon under her pillow.

Her expression must have changed because Sean's eyes narrowed. "What is it?"

"Hello, on the mountain!" At a yell from above, they tilted their heads to peer through the snow above them and she avoided Sean's question.

A neon-green snowsuit announced Tyler's arrival. The kid raced down the mountain with the reckless fearlessness of youth. He ripped over a hummock, executed some kind of fancy jump, then slid to a hair-raising stop amid a spray of snow from his skis.

Tyler waved his ski pole in greeting. "Isn't this corn snow fabulous?"

"Corn snow?" Carlie asked, unfamiliar with the term and trying to regain her equilibrium after Sean's devastating kiss.

"It's snow that's melted then refrozen into clusters of tiny ice balls," Tyler explained with enthusiasm. "It's a fairly decent surface for skiing."

"Yeah, terrific," Sean grumbled, seemingly dismissing the effects of her kiss with no effort.

Surely he must have felt some of the smoldering heat they'd shared. Her heart still pounded. Yet to look at him standing with his feet solidly spread, his shoulders relaxed and his face stoic, he might have already forgotten her.

Sean focused his gaze on Tyler. "Seen anyone around? Any tracks?"

Tyler raised his goggles to his forehead, planted his ski poles into the snow and leaned on them, breathing heavily. "Just you two, why?" He spotted the snowmobile lying on its side and frowned. "Wow. Have an accident? Are you guys okay?"

"We're fine," Carlie told him, drawing Tyler's attention to her.

"Get you memory back, ma'am?"

She discounted the vague recollections of a blond-haired man. While it was kind of him to ask about her, her instincts went on alert. Jackson's killer would be very interested in what she did or did not remember.

While Sean hiked up to the tree and unhooked the death trap, Carlie changed the subject. "Someone strung a wire between those trees."

Tyler raised his hand to his neck and moved it from left to right.

Carlie nodded. "You got the picture."

Tyler swallowed hard and looked fearfully at the wire. "If I had taken the left trail…"

"It might have sliced you in half." Sean removed the wire from the second spruce and joined them. "There are tracks up there."

"Can you read them?" Tyler asked, his eyes bright and curious.

"Can't tell much. I'd say our guy is one hundred and fifty to two hundred pounds, right-handed, with a shoe size between ten and twelve. He's not good in the woods.''

He knew all that from a few smudged footprints? But this was his territory. He was lord of this mountain. Impressed with his knowledge but a tad skeptical, Carlie asked, ''How can you tell?''

''I had to estimate weight and shoe size because snow filled in most of the footprints. I'm guessing right-handed because of the direction he twisted the wire.''

''And how do you know he's not good in the woods?'' Carlie asked.

''He slipped around a lot. The edges of the tracks were soft. A mountain man would have worn cleats, even snowshoes to hike up here.''

Tyler looked at Sean with admiration. ''Damn, you're awesome. Can you follow the trail?''

Sean shook his head. ''In another fifteen minutes, the tracks will be completely covered.'' He turned toward the snowmobile. ''I can use some help, getting her turned over.''

Carlie and Tyler followed him. Carlie noticed Tyler didn't even take off his skis. The kid was so agile, the skis were almost a part of him.

Taking the heaviest end, Sean stood near the front of the vehicle. Tyler joined him at the rear and Carlie stood between them.

''On three,'' Sean directed. ''One, two, three.''

Carlie heaved, throwing her weight into the heavy machine. Beside her, Sean grunted. Tyler's face turned red.

Slowly, the snowmobile turned upright.

Tyler cast a worried frown at the darkening sky. "Think she'll start?"

Sean dusted snow off the seat. "Now that she's upright, we'll give the engine a few minutes to drain." He checked his instrumentation, then glanced from the sky to Tyler. "You're welcome to spend the night."

"No, thanks." Tyler pulled his goggles from his forehead to cover his eyes. "I've got a date."

He waited until Sean choked and started the motor, then shoved himself down the mountain. Within ten seconds, he'd vanished as if he'd never been there.

Relief filled Carlie at the sound of the purring engine. She didn't relish the thought of walking through the gusting snow. Climbing on the seat behind Sean, remembering his reluctance for any physical contact, she hesitated to put her arms around his waist. Despite his emotional withdrawal, she still sensed a redolent sexuality in his movements but couldn't understand why she felt that way, except that the last time they were so close, he had been kissing her. And he'd pushed her away. She didn't want to touch him again, but how else could she hold on? Finally she grabbed two fistfuls of his snowsuit at his waist.

He turned his head and spoke over his shoulder. "I'm going to take her real slow—just in case there are any other surprises out here."

Unwilling to dwell on what had happened during or after their kiss, she forced her thoughts back to their predicament. "Does anyone use this trail except you?"

"Maybe the occasional hunter."

Roger, Tyler and Marvin, the three men on the mountain the day of Jackson's death, were all between one hundred fifty and two hundred pounds. But for that matter so were the banker and Sean. "Do you happen to know whether Tyler is right- or left-handed?"

"Why?"

"Did you see any ski tracks around the wire?"

He shook his head. "Doesn't mean they weren't there, though. With weight distributed along a six-foot ski as opposed to concentrated in a boot, the tracks would have been light and filled in quickly." He paused. "Surely you don't suspect Tyler could have set the wire?"

"I suspect everyone." At the slow speed, conversation was almost intimate over the soft hum of the engine. "Tyler works in the mine for you as well as for Ian Finley at the bank, right?"

"So?"

"Why two jobs?"

"He has dreams of Olympic glory. In the summer when there's no snow, he works in the mine. And in winter, he only works part-time in the bank. He's hoping to make the national ski team next year and needs practice time on the slopes."

"He only works part-time all winter? That's not much to live on."

"He wouldn't have to work, except that before his father died, he lost the mining stock he'd inherited in a poker game. He lives in his father's cabin."

She ignored the residual heat from Sean's kiss, her anger and hurt at his rejection of her, and kept her tone businesslike. "So Tyler had the means and opportunity to kill Jackson, but I don't see a motive. Did Tyler have any reason to be angry with Jackson?''

Sean shrugged. ''He's an odd kid, always popping up on the mountain where you least expect him. Jackson tried to be nice to him.''

''But?''

''He and Jackson got along fine.'' Sean was holding something back, but clearly he was unwilling to say more.

Sensing she would have more luck wringing a confession out of a stone than making Sean say more than he wanted to, she changed the subject. ''What about Roger? Would he have had time to set the wire, then catch up with us at Jackson's cabin?''

''Sure. And Marvin could have left the warm gambling hall and climbed up here during the storm. Everyone in Kesky knows this trail.''

Great, so anyone could have strung the wire. Anyone could have sighted the rifle on her. Anyone could have killed Jackson. But only her prints were on the murder weapon. Her sleeve had been the one stained with his blood. Carlie gritted her teeth. Was it just her imagination, or was Sean deliberately trying to confuse her?

DESPITE THE SNOWSTORM, Carlie had insisted on the snowmobile trip into Kesky the next morning. Sean decided to take her to the general store to pick up a few changes of clothes, and then over lunch, he'd tell her the truth and finally explain they weren't married. Perhaps then she would get over her annoyance for him for treating her with gentlemanly restraint. And understand why he wasn't free to take the liberties she offered. He'd kissed her. So what? He had to forget the kiss. Forget how good her curves felt beneath him. Problem was he couldn't forget it. No matter how often he told himself he'd had no right to steal that kiss, he'd wanted more.

Fessing up to his lie would put more distance between them. Distance he needed. He'd spent a tense, uncomfortable night and deserved to suffer after he'd promised himself not to touch her.

Like an itch that he couldn't leave alone, his thoughts kept returning to their kiss, the memory making his jeans uncomfortable. He should have resisted her. But when he remembered how wonderfully worried about him she'd been he couldn't help his reaction. He was only human. With flaws. From the first moment he'd met her he'd lied to her. Getting the secret off his chest would be a relief after the tense hours in the cabin last night.

He shouldn't have kissed her. But how could he resist when she'd looked sexy as sin with her golden hair spilling out from beneath her hat, her eyes brimming with concern? He'd responded on instinct, her distress touching him on a level far deeper than the mere sexual. Her kiss had been fiery and passionate, and she kissed with the same powerful intensity that so often showed in her expressive eyes.

For a moment he'd forgotten he had no right to share those passions. She wasn't his wife, but rather his best friend's widow, and soon she would know of Sean's deception. He only hoped after he told her the truth she would understand his obligation to Bill and his need to protect her. While he had no doubt she could protect herself in her own territory, out here she wasn't prepared for what she might come up against.

He drew the snowmobile to a stop at the town's edge, trying to imagine the place through her eyes. First impressions of Kesky would strike most newcomers as desolate. The ramshackle town looked straight out of a tourist's worst nightmare.

Kesky's forefathers had laid out the town along the Kuskwin River, and many of the buildings stood tall on stilts. Others sat, henlike, on oversize water and sewer tanks that had been coated with spray-on foam insulation.

There were no city conveniences in Kesky. No cinema or espresso bars. No 7-Eleven. No bookstores. Not even a Dairy Queen. The general store, the closest thing to a gift shop, sold a few religious trinkets, clothing and groceries. The largest hotel in town, the Kuskwin Inn, closed five years ago after the roof collapsed, and it showed no sign of reopening.

The most conspicuous piece of architecture was the Kesky National Bank, a rambling marigold-colored monstrosity with round windows. Locals affectionately called Ian's bank the Yellow Submarine.

Carlie's eyes widened as they parked the snowmobile and walked down the one-street town. "What are those tubes?"

"Sidewalks." He kept waiting for a snide remark about how primitive they were, but she seemed more fascinated than horrified so he explained further. "About half the buildings in Kesky are linked via those above-ground aluminum ducts. It beats shoveling snow or fighting the mud come spring.''

"Clever." She looked up and down the street. "Where would I find a pay phone?"

"The general store." His stomach churned. He'd have to tell her about his deception soon. "Once you give him the phone number, Andrew, the manager, will place the call for you. Sometimes it takes a while to get through. We can wait in the sandwich shop until he gets a connection."

He hoped the restaurant would be empty so he could explain his deception in privacy. Surely she would understand he'd lied to protect her. But if the facts were so self-evident, then why were his nerves so jumpy?

He watched as she strode inside with eager steps, pushing past the inventory of down jackets, gloves and toques. The scents of tanned leather, wood smoke and people assaulted his nostrils. He followed slowly but didn't let her out of his sight, fairly certain someone wanted her dead. He couldn't forget the attempts on her life. Between the gun sighted on her shoulder and the wire strung in the woods, he was sure someone wanted her out of the way before she regained her memory. And that someone had to be Jackson's murderer. Because once Carlie's memory returned, she could identify the killer.

Sean would have preferred staying on the relatively remote mountain, his territory, where he could protect her more easily. In the woods, he could hear a man trying to sneak up on him. If the wind blew from the right direction, he would catch his scent.

Animals gave their own warnings, terns, warblers and puffin lifting to the sky if disturbed by man.

Thanks to hours in the mountains hunting and fishing with Jackson, the wire strung across his path yesterday had immediately caught his attention, the copper standing out against the gray sky. Nature didn't provide such straight edges. To him, the trap signaled like a road sign.

But in town with people coming and going, protecting Carlie became more difficult. Tiny Kesky, with a population of about one hundred, presented different dangers, new opportunities for whoever wanted Carlie out of the way.

His vigilance inched up another notch. He reminded himself she wore a weapon and that she knew how to use it. Gazing to his right, his left, then straight ahead, he took in a few customers shopping in the canned goods section, others in the cramped restaurant.

Carlie made a beeline for the lunch counter, Andrew and the phone. The store manager greeted her with a wary nod. "Carlie, what can I do for you?"

"You know my name?"

"You introduced yourself a few days ago."

Carlie looked at Andrew carefully, taking in his huge belly and the apron he wore over it. "I don't remember."

Andrew scowled at her. "Heard about your memory loss. You came here looking for Sean. I told you he had a meeting with Jackson at the mine and you said you'd meet him at the Dog Mush."

"Did I say anything else?"

"I don't recall. I was going to send someone up

to Sean's cabin, but with the storm, I forgot.'' Andrew opened a door in the back room and pointed to a knapsack and a suitcase. ''You'll be wanting your things.''

''Thanks, Andrew,'' Sean said. ''Mind holding them for a few hours more?''

''No problem.''

As anxious as she appeared to retrieve the belongings she didn't seem to recognize, she didn't protest the wait. While Sean had no wish to tote the luggage around while they were in town, his other reason was equally practical. He wanted to tell her of his deception in private and the restaurant was too crowded. He couldn't let her go through her luggage until he could explain why he'd deceived her. He didn't need mementos of her past reminding her that she wasn't his wife until he had her safely back at his cabin.

Carlie drummed her fingers on the countertop. ''How long will it take to place a call to Florida?''

Andrew chewed on a toothpick and shrugged his beefy shoulders. ''Sorry. Storm knocked out Alascom.''

''Alascom?''

''Alaska's major long distance telephone service provider. Could be a day or two before service is restored.''

Carlie bit her bottom lip, her disappointment obvious. ''A day or two?''

''Yep.''

Relief flooded Sean. He wouldn't have to tell her about his lie. Not today.

''Can I send a fax?''

Andrew shot her a funny look. ''Phone line, fax

line, it's still the same wires. And it's the wires that are down.''

"The entire town has only one line?''

Andrew nodded.

"And no one has a cell phone?''

Sean tensed at the incredulity underlying her questions. He had already explained to her about cell phones. Either she didn't trust him and doubted his word or she'd forgotten. And somehow he didn't think she'd forgotten. Except for the two years she'd lost due to her amnesia, she seemed sharp as a fox and twice as edgy.

"Oh, sure lots of us have cell phones." Andrew gestured with his toothpick to one on the counter.

Carlie's eyes lit with pleasure. "Could I borrow that? I'd be willing to call collect and—''

"Won't do you any good," Andrew explained. "Mountains block the transmissions.''

"Then why do you have cell phones at all?" Carlie asked, obviously frustrated.

"We use them when we leave Kesky," Sean told her gently. "Or when we fly our planes.''

"Kesky has an airport?''

Andrew let out a loud snort, signaled for Sean to answer her and moved on to help another customer.

Sean started to lead the way to a booth in the restaurant. "We use seaplanes and the river provides us with a runway.''

"Hey, I almost forgot." Andrew hurried to catch up with them. "Sally left you a message.''

The store manager pulled slips of paper from his pocket and started to sort through them. Finally he frowned. "Can't seem to find it. But she said whenever you hit town to come by and to bring your wife. She'll fix you a meal."

Carlie looked up at him, her eyebrows drawn together in puzzlement. "How'd Sally know we married? How'd she know we were coming to town?"

Andrew choked back another snort. "In Kesky everybody knows everyone's business. Within two hours of Roger, Marvin and Tyler coming down that mountain, the entire population, from Mary's two-year-old Quinn to ninety-one-year-old Daisy Mae knew you two married. We may not have a great phone system, but that doesn't mean we don't talk." Letting out a full chuckle, Andrew walked away.

At the same moment, Wayne Riker, one of the few residents of Kesky that Sean didn't like, hurried around a rack of clothes, almost tripping Carlie with his diamond willow walking stick. Dressed in an Alaskan tuxedo—a slacks-and-jacket ensemble of wool whipcord that somewhat resembled a heavy-duty leisure suit—he reminded Sean of a peacock. Despite his dislike of the man, Wayne was a great quartermaster and Sean had kept him on the mine's payroll.

Wayne reached out past his bulging stomach to steady Carlie. "Whoops. Sorry about that."

Carlie regained her footing. "It's okay."

"You must be Sean's wife." Wayne leaned on his walking stick and pumped Carlie's hand with a false joviality that grated on Sean's nerves. "Wayne Riker. I'm the camp quartermaster." He winked. "And if there's anything you need that you can't find, feel free to look me up."

"I'll do that," Carlie said as the man issued a wave and took off into the store.

Sean knew their conversation would be discussed all over town by noon. Maybe he should have warned her. Without television, without radio or a movie theater, Kesky's main entertainment was gossip.

He gave Carlie ten minutes to shop before his impatience urged her out of the store.

When the saleswoman finally left Carlie alone for a moment, he stepped to her side. "You going to talk all day?"

Sally's invitation complemented Sean's plan to leave town as soon as possible. There were too many people coming and going. Although Sally lived on the edge of Kesky, Sean knew they'd be safe there.

Carlie gave him a curious look. "What's the hurry?"

"Sally makes the best Eskimo ice cream," he told her, deliberately keeping his voice light.

"You expect me to believe all your rushing is due to a sweet tooth?"

"Believe what you wish."

Although Sean expected everyone who saw them to stop and meet his wife, he found the population avoided them and he realized many people must blame her for Jackson's murder. In town, she was exposed, vulnerable. But any newcomer created interest. He had to remind himself repeatedly that not every day did a man marry a woman who turned out to be a suspected murderer.

As they strolled down the street, curtains lifted, eyes peered out of windows. Refusing to allow Carlie's obvious interest in the town and its residents to slow them, Sean urged her to walk more quickly.

Instinct told him Carlie was too exposed on the street. He couldn't protect her out in the open. And the hunter in him sensed a malevolent presence following their every step.

But when he turned around to look, he couldn't see a threat.

Chapter Seven

Sally lived in a stilt house, just on the edge of town. Snow clung to the steep A-frame roof and the occasional icicle, heating in the noonday sun, broke off and splashed into the Kuskwin River under her front porch. Otters swam busily and muskrats played along the banks.

Uncomfortable with the idea of dropping in unexpectedly for a lunch with a stranger, Carlie dawdled. Sean seemed to have no such qualms. In fact he seemed so eager to reach the house that Carlie wondered what Sally meant to him. Was she a substitute mother? From Sean's tone of voice whenever he spoke about the woman, Carlie knew he admired her.

Sean led Carlie up the steps and knocked on the door. When the door opened, the first thing Carlie noticed was the woman's height.

While Sean and Sally hugged, each consoling the other over Jackson's death, Carlie removed her jacket and then took the opportunity to stare at the other woman. At five foot nine, Carlie thought of herself as tall, but Sally, in pink fuzzy slippers and matching sequinned robe, stood at least six foot two. Shoulders squared, back straight, her impeccable posture showed off enormous breasts. But most surprising of all was that the woman with auburn wavy hair cut stylishly short had to be in her mid-fifties.

"About time you paid your respects," she snapped after pulling away from Sean. Her eyes filled with tears. "I miss Jackson so much."

"Me, too," Sean agreed.

Carlie shifted from foot to foot, the floorboards creaking beneath her feet. Feeling the outsider, she wanted to leave. As the suspected murderer, she felt more than uncomfortable.

Carlie started to put her jacket back on. "If this is a bad time—"

"These days, any time is a good time. We never know how much we have left." Sally took Carlie's coat, then seized her hands with surprising strength and looked straight into her eyes.

"Well?" Sean asked, his face giving nothing away, but she heard the affectionate amusement in his tone.

"Strong, stubborn and smart." Sally spoke slowly, her voice crisp with approval for whatever she'd read in Carlie's face. The flamboyant woman turned Carlie's palms over and tugged her toward a light. "Don't be bashful, child."

Carlie pulled her hands free and stuck them in her pocket. She hadn't come here to have her fortune told, didn't believe in the supernatural.

Carlie tried to speak with diplomacy. "I'd prefer not to know the future."

Instead of taking insult, Sally looked down her

long nose at her and broke into a wide smile. "I *knew* she was strong." Gesturing them to follow, she glided forward in her slippers, her head high as a queen's, and led them into an immaculate kitchen with a shiny linoleum floor. "Come inside while I fix us some lunch."

A man sat at her kitchen table, sipping bourbon.

Marvin? The gambler. Surely Sally didn't still ply her trade. Sean had indicated that Sally and Jackson had had a special relationship, so Carlie hadn't expected to find the gambler here this soon after Jackson's death.

Marvin raised his glass in greeting, his gold tooth winking. "Good afternoon." A deck of playing cards rested on the table beside a pad of paper where he'd obviously been keeping score of their card game.

Without turning his head, Sean glanced from Marvin to Sally and back. "Didn't expect to see him here."

Sally reached into the refrigerator and her robes slipped, revealing a delicate tattoo of a rose on her shoulder. "A girl gets lonely. Jackson spent most of his time in the mine. He knew Marvin and I played gin."

Carlie wondered what else they played together. A glance at Sean didn't give her a clue to his thoughts. As usual, he didn't make any fidgety or restless movements. He didn't tap his foot or drum his fingers. He simply commanded the area he occupied.

Marvin shoved back his chair and stood. "I'd best be moving along, anyways."

Sean didn't move from his spot in the doorway. "Mind telling us where you were yesterday?"

His poker face inscrutable, Marvin picked up the cards and placed them in a box. "When?"

"Between ten and three."

Carlie figured the deadly copper wire had to have been strung after the banker and Roger left Sean's home and before she and Sean had returned from Roger's cabin.

"I was sleeping."

"Where?" Sean asked.

"My place."

"You slept all day?" Carlie asked.

"I play poker all night if the game is a good one. Roger dropped a bundle."

"And you cleaned up?" Sean asked.

"Lady Luck was sitting on my lap."

Carlie sniffed appreciatively as Sally melted butter in a cast-iron pan and tossed in diced onions. "Can anyone verify that you were asleep?"

Marvin shook his head. "Last I heard, sleeping alone wasn't a crime."

"Do you own a gun with a laser sight?" Carlie asked.

"Haven't fired her in years."

Sean reached over Sally's counter and helped himself to a slice of cheese. "Been in the woods lately?"

"I don't have to answer your questions, you know."

"Humor me."

"First tell me where you're going with all these questions."

Carlie watched Marvin's eyes. 'We're trying to eliminate you as a murder suspect.''

He didn't flinch at her not-so-subtle accusation. She suspected he was one hell of a poker player.

Marvin's voice stayed even. "Eliminate me? Why would I want to kill Jackson? He owed me money."

"For what?" Carlie asked.

"My share in the mine."

Carlie tried to keep track of the various mine's owners. The banker and Sean each owned forty-five percent shares. Roger and Marvin each owned two percent. She wondered who the other two percent owners were.

Marvin held his hands out to her, his tone steady, his eyes calm. "I'd have no reason to want him dead." He sounded the voice of reason. "Now that Jackson's not running the Dog Mush, the mine may not run as profitably, especially—" his eyes moved from Sean to Carlie "—since he has other interests on his mind."

Sean's words had a hard edge. "You'll get your money." He turned to Sally, "Both of you will."

So Sally also owned two percent of the mine, Carlie thought. That left only two more partial owners— but she supposed it didn't matter. What had Marvin upset was that Sean was helping her instead of running his business. But she'd gotten the impression that the miners didn't work in the winter once the ground had frozen. Perhaps she should insist Sean go back to work and let her investigate on her own. But she doubted he would listen.

While Kesky's entire economy didn't depend on the mine, guilt stabbed her that men would lose wages because of her. Until now she hadn't once thought of the consequences of taking all of Sean's time with her investigation.

Sean pulled out a chair and straddled it. "The men can't travel up the mountain in this weather and you know it. We may as well close up for the winter."

Now that his escape route was clear, Marvin exchanged a look with Sally. Sally shook her head at him, answering some unspoken question, and he headed for the door. "I'll see myself out."

Sally waited until Marvin left, then turned on Sean. "You weren't very friendly. Marvin's asked me to marry him."

Sean didn't move. He didn't tense. His expression didn't change, and yet Carlie could almost feel anger radiating off of him. After several silent seconds passed, he finally spoke. "What did you say?"

"Yes. I told him yes. We filled out the license this morning and our paperwork should be ready in three days."

Three days to complete the paperwork? Carlie tucked that interesting fact into the back of her mind.

"Didn't expect you to replace Jackson before we even buried him."

"Sean!" Carlie didn't like the harsh tone he used with the woman.

Hands trembling, Sally flipped the grilled cheese sandwiches onto plates and placed them on the table. All three of them ignored the food.

Sally looked Sean straight in the eye. "I miss Jackson, Sean. I could take ten men into my bed and there'd still be a big hole in my heart where Jackson used to be, and no one's ever going to fill it like he did.''

At the woman's plea for understanding, Carlie thought Sean would soften. But he didn't. He didn't budge. He said nothing.

Sean stared at the woman. She stared back. The food grew cold.

Could Marvin have murdered Jackson so he could propose to Sally? Carlie didn't know. And with the tension so high, she didn't dare ask.

Finally Carlie had to break the strained silence. ''Did Jackson have any enemies?''

''Not that I know about.'' Sally helped herself to a sandwich that she shredded into pieces, not once putting a morsel in her mouth.

''Did he seem worried about anything?''

Sally shook her head. ''He seemed excited.''

''About?'' Sean prodded.

''He went up on the mountain to meet you that morning to tell you the good news. Recent assay reports suggest the Dog Mush is about to hit the mother lode.''

DURING LUNCH, CARLIE had sampled Eskimo ice cream, a concoction of whipped berries, sugar and freshly fallen snow, but she'd learned nothing further to help solve her murder investigation. She'd questioned Sally, who couldn't think of any reason someone would want Jackson dead. Jackson's hope that the mine would strike a rich vein didn't seem a motive for murder—not when the rich vein had yet to be found. A jealous lover seemed more likely a motive—yet Marvin didn't seem the violent type.

Although the meal had ended on a pleasant note, Carlie couldn't forget Sean's harsh words and harsher judgment. While the former prostitute had appeared to forgive him, Carlie couldn't. What right did he have to judge how the woman should grieve or for how long she grieved? Or who she spent her time with now?

His severe condemnation of Sally revealed an aspect of Sean's character she didn't understand or like. But then she didn't know Sean McCabe well. He never spoke about his past.

He shut Sally's door behind them and took Carlie's elbow as they strode down the slippery steps. "I wouldn't put too much credence in Jackson's hope of the Dog Mush striking a rich vein."

"Why?" She glanced at his serious expression, noting the way the light angled off the slant of his cheekbones, his face appearing hard as chiseled onyx.

"Jackson was a dreamer."

"Everyone speaks well of him." She dared a personal question. "What kind of father was he?"

Sean stopped on the steps and stared out at Kisku Mountain, which threw a long shadow over the town. For a long time, she didn't think Sean would answer her, but finally he turned and looked into her eyes.

"Jackson was the best father a kid could have. Even after a hard week in the mine, on weekends, he always had time to take me rock climbing, fishing or hunting. The only thing he owned of value was the Dog Mush. But he gave me half of his share and then mortgaged his part to send me to college."

She could hear in his softened tone how much he

loved the old prospector. "How did you come to live with him?"

Sean threaded his hand through his dark hair, an uncharacteristic movement revealing how uncomfortable this conversation made him. "You're very perceptive."

Puzzled, she took his hand and walked down the rest of the steps. As if of one mind, they strolled along the river away from town, disturbing a slow-moving porcupine who waddled from the banks into a stand of black cottonwood.

"Me, perceptive? I don't understand."

"Sure you do. You want to know why I came down so hard on Sally and figure it must have something to do with my past."

Her mouth dropped open in surprise. She'd thought she was being so subtle, but he'd caught on to her almost immediately.

"Well, you're probably right," he continued without any additional prodding from her. "My biological father was a trapper and an alcoholic. He headed off one day and never returned. My mother died six months later. I was eight years old. Jackson took me in before social services caught up with me."

Carlie realized he was telling her the most abbreviated of versions about his past. A father's unexplained disappearance must have been hard on a young child. And then to lose his mother, too. Her heart went out to the little boy he'd been, but she kept the emotion tamped down inside. The man next to her wanted no pity.

And she still didn't understand why he'd condemned Sally earlier. Sally's marrying Marvin couldn't hurt Jackson now.

"How did you and your mother survive after your father left?" she asked.

Sean stopped along the river, searched out a few flat rocks at the bank where water had melted away the snow, and skipped the stones across the water. Below them beavers had dammed one side of the river. Gurgling water, tall Alaskan cedar reflected on the rippling surface and the fresh scent of snow lent an air of privacy to the conversation.

"My mother took men into her bed to put food in my mouth."

"And you condemn her—"

"On the contrary. I hated what my father did to my mother, that he'd left her in such a state that she had no choice." He turned to face her. "When Jackson died, I made sure Sally knew she would be cared for. Roger carried down the message from me. Sally has a choice."

Carlie heard the pain and frustration in his tone. While she suspected Sally didn't want charity, that wasn't what he needed to hear. Sean needed comforting and she searched for the words to ease his pain.

Carlie reached for his hand. "Maybe—"

Sean pulled away. "She doesn't need to—"

"I read somewhere that when a much-loved partner dies, the survivor often replaces that person almost immediately. To outsiders it seems cold, callous. But the survivor can't bear to be alone because he or she so badly misses the one who died."

His expression darkened. "That's needy."

She thought of the good times she remembered with her mother, her father and her sister. What she wouldn't give to have them here with her now, hugging her, helping her sort out her feelings. Out of nowhere, the blond man's face popped into her mind. Somehow he'd been important in her life, too.

She twisted her hands together. "There's nothing wrong with needing people."

His eyes narrowed with bitterness and pain. "Needing my father killed my mother. As sorry an excuse for a human being as he was, she couldn't survive without him."

"But you did."

"Jackson taught me to survive."

Jackson had taught him to rely on himself. The old prospector had done a fine job, Carlie thought sarcastically. Sean was strong, independent, a loner very much satisfied with his own company. But what made him strong also made him afraid to let her in. That's why he rarely spoke about anything personal. That's why he didn't like to be touched. He didn't want to need a woman because she might leave him as his mother had, as Jackson had.

As she might. She could be going to jail. Or she might head back to Florida. Something that Sean had told her didn't sit quite right. According to his story, they'd met and married on the same day—but the paperwork from the state took three days. The facts didn't add up. Damn it, she wished she had her memories. Had she really married this man after exchanging only a few letters?

They had little in common. And yet she couldn't deny that every time she thought about the kiss they'd shared, heat sparked through her and contentment glowed warmly deep in her middle. Desire surged between them, a current as swift and sure as the raging river. But no matter how sexy she found him, she knew herself well enough to know that she wouldn't have married a man because she wanted to make love to him.

"Sally said the paperwork to obtain a license takes three days."

"So?"

"You told me we married the same day we met."

"And I explained that I pulled a few strings."

He stared at the river as if lost in thought. Or was he disturbed that she obviously questioned his former explanation? Looking at his stonelike expression told her nothing.

She needed answers. She needed her memories. Without the missing part of herself, she could go no further. She'd run out of questions to ask. And he wasn't volunteering any more information. Cold seeped into her boots and she couldn't restrain a shiver.

Sean, ever-observant, took her by the arm. "I've kept you out here too long. We'll retrieve your luggage and then head back to the cabin."

Once she started walking, she warmed right up. Instinct told her he'd lied to her, and she couldn't shake the lingering sense of unease. They returned to the general store with her still trying to put her gloomy thoughts behind her.

The store was busier than during their first visit, but in no way did it replace the pleasures of shopping at her local mall with its myriad of shops. What she wouldn't give for a golden box of Godiva chocolate. While the atmosphere here was friendly, it didn't include her. Women shopped and visited, their youngsters playing tag among the barrels of grocery staples. Men congregated at the luncheon tables.

Marvin sat at a poker table but threw in his hand at the sight of Sean and Carlie in the store. He left his stack of chips without a second glance. Carlie watched with trepidation as the gambler approached.

He tipped back his hat and squared his shoulders. "I didn't kill Jackson so I could marry Sally."

"No one's saying you did." Sean didn't move. He didn't blink or shrug or indicate the conversation made him uncomfortable in any way. Instead he simply controlled his space by his mere presence in it.

While Carlie held her breath, the gambler held Sean's gaze for a full minute. Finally, he tipped his hat. "You know where to find me if you want me."

Andrew, a toothpick drooping from the corner of his mouth, retrieved her suitcase, and she swung the backpack over her shoulder. Hoping familiar items might give her some clues to her missing memories, she couldn't wait to explore her luggage and secretly hoped she'd stashed some chocolate inside to fortify her.

CARLIE HELPED SEAN park the snowmobile in his shed. He picked up her suitcase, a resigned look in his eyes as she shouldered her backpack. While she could barely contain her eagerness to look through her things, she still noticed Sean's rigid silence.

He hadn't spoken since they'd left Kesky, and she wondered if he was still disturbed by Sally's coming marriage to Marvin. Suspecting your friends of murder had to be troubling. Marvin had had the means, a motive and an opportunity. The gambler had been on the mountain with Tyler and Roger. Marvin seemed familiar with weapons. And he was about to marry Jackson's lady friend.

Yet, Roger was just as much a suspect. Jackson's brother was strong as an ox and she suspected he could wield a knife with ease. And he'd inherited Jackson's cabin.

She reminded herself not to forget Tyler. He'd grown up in these parts and probably had weapons. But so far, she couldn't find a motive for the kid to have murdered the old prospector.

Jackson's murder need not have been committed by one of her suspects. Anyone could have been on the mountain and then hightailed it to town without having been seen. It didn't take much strength to stab an old man in the chest. Even Sally could have done it during a lover's quarrel.

Carlie entered Sean's cabin and swung the backpack off her shoulder. Without more facts, her speculations weren't going far. A tremble of fear shimmied down her at the thought that her memory might never return.

Settle down.

Maybe an object in her backpack would trigger a recollection of those missing two years. After removing her jacket and boots, she wandered into the bedroom and dumped the contents of the backpack on the bed.

Sean wandered in with her suitcase, his enigmatic

eyes seemingly reconciled to whatever she might find. "I'll start dinner."

Carlie sifted through a cosmetics bag, assorted toiletries and two paperback mysteries. She found a daybook with Sean's name and post office box in Kesky scribbled on the front page but no chocolate. In a side pocket nestled two credit cards, traveling money and her driver's license. Curious, she stared at her picture.

Staring back at her was the same face she'd seen in the mirror this morning, and yet she didn't remember when she'd had the picture taken. Carlie checked the date. Almost a year and a half ago. Why couldn't she remember?

She swallowed the lump in her throat, determined not to feel sorry for herself. She was about to toss the license back into the zippered pocket when her name caught her eye.

Carlie Myer.

But her last name was Brandon!

An eerie feeling made the hair on the back of her neck prickle. With shaking fingers, she picked up the two credit cards. Both had Carlie Myer embossed in the hard plastic.

Her gaze focused on the plain gold band on her ring finger of her left hand. Confusion coursed through her veins. She didn't understand what she'd found but knew Sean couldn't have been straight with her—not unless she'd lied to him.

Could she have married Sean without telling him that she was already married? Or maybe she'd married and divorced and hadn't had time to change her driver's license since marrying Sean.

With her stomach churning, Carlie searched the rest of the backpack. She found extra ammunition for her gun and a permit to carry the weapon—still in the name of Myer—but nothing else that might help with the puzzle of her last name.

With reluctance she turned to her suitcase, almost dreading what she would find. But as she unpacked the clothing she didn't recognize, she found no further clues to the mystery.

"Anything ring a bell?" Sean poked his head in the door, his tone casual, almost too casual. Or was her imagination working overtime? The intensity in his eyes caused her to wonder how much he knew about her that he wasn't telling.

Reluctant to reveal what she had found, she nevertheless answered his question truthfully. "This is so frustrating. I have no recollection of any of these items except buying these socks."

His tone softened. "It'll come back to you. Don't force it. Meantime, the bottom drawers are empty and you can have the right side of the closet."

"Thanks." She wondered if he could hear the trembling in her voice.

He turned away, speaking over his shoulder. "I've got to check the burgers. Supper will be ready in about fifteen minutes."

Sean seemed so much more reserved than usual, as if he almost expected her to find something and hold it against him. But what? She couldn't blame him that she no longer used her maiden name.

Needing the comfort of an everyday task to restore her frazzled nerves, Carlie folded her clothes and put them away. She sniffed one nubby sweater, hoping it might bring back a memory. Instead, her head pounded with the futile effort.

She hadn't brought much with her, maybe enough for a two-week vacation. But for all she knew, she'd shipped the rest and the remainder of her things would arrive shortly.

After tucking the empty suitcase under the bed, Carlie started to toss the toiletries into her backpack. Her finger caught on a scrap of paper at the bottom of her bag.

Gently, she pried the newspaper clipping loose. The blond-haired man of her memories stared back at her. Beneath his picture was his name.

Bill Myer.

The same last name as the one on her driver's license. At some point, she'd been married to the man in the picture. She tried to dredge up one feeling for Bill Myer. But he could have been a stranger.

Her knees weak with shock, she slumped onto the bed. She was married to someone named Myer. And Sean's last name was McCabe.

Chapter Eight

Carlie didn't say one word to Sean during dinner about what she'd discovered in her backpack. She put food in her mouth and chewed as if on autopilot. But from the anger glittering in her eyes, the defiant set of her chin and the rigid set of her shoulders, he concluded that she knew he'd lied to her.

She had a fire started in the fireplace when he joined her. But the flames couldn't match the furious blaze in her eyes. "We aren't married, are we?"

Sean straddled a chair opposite her. Since the moment Andrew had mentioned her luggage, he'd known this moment was coming. While he could have gone through her things and removed the identification she must have found, he'd refused to compound his lie with additional deceptions.

Jackson would have been disappointed in Sean. The old prospector hadn't approved of lying or taking advantage of women.

And Sean felt even guiltier as he recalled Bill's occasional letter. The man had adored his wife and would have been horrified to know that his Alaskan friend had deceived the woman he'd held in such high esteem.

Carlie Myer was no fool. Over the past few days, he'd come to respect her determination in the face of danger. She'd defended him against Roger. She'd eased his harsh feelings over Sally's seeming betrayal of Jackson's memory. She'd tried to save him from a deadly wire strung in their path, and he'd long since stopped thinking of her as a murder suspect.

With surprise, he realized that she'd become his partner in searching for Jackson's murderer. He no longer felt it necessary to keep her with him under false pretenses. She deserved the truth.

But coming clean was more difficult than he expected. He didn't want to lose her trust. Didn't want to watch her respect for him wither to cold disgust. She sat on the couch with her legs curled beneath her, looking at him warily through long, dark lashes.

He chose his words carefully. "About two years ago, you married my best friend, Bill Myer. You and I'd never met until I found you next to Jackson's body."

"Am I still married?"

He read the anguish in her eyes and cursed himself for putting her through more uncertainty. "You're a widow. Last year, Bill died in an automobile accident. You still don't remember?"

She ignored his question and kept her tone reasonable, but an edge of anger crept in. "Do you know why I came to Alaska?"

"To see me. I assumed you wanted to check on your investment."

She rubbed her palms on her thighs. "What investment?"

"Bill won a small share in the mine from Tyler's father during a poker game."

He thought she would ask how much her share was worth or maybe how much income she would receive, but she didn't question him about money. She had no apparent interest in the mine or her inheritance.

"Why did you tell me we are married?"

"I didn't tell *you*, I told the men." She opened her mouth to protest and he continued, "But I'm splitting hairs. The truth is..."

"What?"

"Complicated."

He leaned forward, wishing he could find the right words to make the past go away. He'd like the opportunity to start fresh, but at least he'd try to undo the mess he'd made. "When I found Jackson, I thought you were dead and had murdered him. You had a knife in your hand, his blood on your sleeve. You awakened and attacked me."

Her eyes widened. "I did?"

"Before you passed out, you told me your name and I knew you were Bill's wife."

"Then you started to have doubts about whether I killed Jackson?"

He nodded, appreciating the logical way her mind worked. Maybe she would accept his explanation. "You were a cop. And I knew Bill well enough to know he was straight-arrow. He wouldn't have married a murderer."

"But you couldn't be sure?"

Her fingers drummed impatiently and he saw that beneath her calm, a storm brewed. He knew that as surely as he knew the difference between fox and bear tracks. Her strong face and indignant eyes told the real story. Even as he tried to assess her, she was sizing him up with a cop's focused intensity and a woman's temper.

He hoped she would understand that he'd acted reasonably once she had all the facts. "I'd already told Marvin over the radio that you were the killer. The men were too angry to think clearly, and I didn't want more violence. You had amnesia and couldn't defend yourself. It occurred to me that whoever killed Jackson might have set you up to take the blame. We all needed time to think."

"But why did you lie about *us?*"

"Those men respect me. While they might tear a stranger limb from limb, they'd give my wife the benefit of the doubt." He paused, no more deceptions. "I also wanted to keep you where I could watch you."

"Why?"

He studied the bold, sculpted planes of her face, her gold hair falling strikingly around her shoulders. The combination of vulnerability and vitality in her expression made it hard for him to look away. He ached to take her into his arms, smooth the worried frown between her delicately arched eyebrows, but she wanted his explanation. When he finished, she might not want him at all. Still, he tried to make her see his reasons.

"I knew if you hadn't killed Jackson, you might be in danger. The best way to protect you was to keep you with me. And after the attempts on your life, it turned out I was right.''

Her eyes searched his, weighing his explanation, but underneath the calm, fury smoldered. ''You've explained why you lied to the men, but why didn't you tell *me* the truth?''

''Would you have moved in with a stranger?''

She raised her chin and squared her shoulders. ''The decision was mine to make.''

Fury at his deception shot from her eyes. For a moment he regretted giving her gun back to her, afraid she might pull it on him. But she had too much self-control. She let out a sigh and closed her eyes as if she could shut him out.

Shoving to his feet, he walked to the sofa. She opened her eyes as he sat beside her and took her hand. ''If I'd known you as well as I do now, I would have been certain you'd make the right decision.''

''Pul—ease.'' She jerked away from him and paced from the fireplace to the hall. ''Don't try and soften me up with flattery.''

He should have known better. ''You were a stranger. You almost left the cabin when you learned I didn't have a phone. I wanted to keep Bill's widow safe.''

Light from the fire reflected off her tanned skin, taut with anger. Hurt mixed with rage and shook her voice. ''You shouldn't have lied to me.''

''If I had to do it all over again, with the facts I have now, I wouldn't have. I wanted to protect you.''

She spun on her heel, fisted her hands on her hips. ''Damn you, I can protect myself. You had no right to deceive me.''

He stood and reached for her hand. "I'm sorry."

She avoided his touch and pointed a finger at his chest. "Sorry doesn't make up for your lies. Sorry doesn't make up for the hurt I felt in believing my own husband could think me capable of murder. Sorry doesn't make up for how you withdrew every time I touched you. No wonder you acted like you were made of stone. We were strangers. And that's how you treated me."

"We *were* strangers—"

She tightened her fingers in a reflexive movement, her too-bright eyes flashing up at him. "But I *thought* we were married. Did it ever occur to you how I felt when you rejected your wife? When you apologized for kissing me?"

The thought of hurting her made nausea rise hot and bitter in his throat. Had he done more harm than he'd imagined? He recalled all the times she'd tried to touch him and how he'd pulled away, thinking he was being noble not to take advantage of her. And every time he'd hurt her.

While she'd required such intimacies from her husband—he'd acted like a stranger. Because of his lie, she'd expected more from him. When he gave her what she wanted on a reckless whim, giving in to the urge to touch the curve of her cheek, exploring the smooth, silky texture of her skin, tasting her lush lips, she'd responded ardently. And after he'd finally gone and kissed her, he'd told her it was a mistake.

He'd already apologized once and was at a loss what to do. "I don't know what to say."

"Then this conversation is over." She walked into

the bedroom, her head high, closing the door quietly behind her.

A log in the fireplace shifted and hissed, but he still heard the harsh click as she turned the lock.

CARLIE TOSSED THE COVERS off and stretched the kink out of her neck. Although Sean's alarm clock read only five-thirty, she couldn't sleep. She'd hoped her memories would return with Sean's explanation, but they hadn't. Instead she'd gone over and over their conversation until she wanted to scream.

How dare he twist her into knots? When he'd finally kissed her, she did what she'd wanted to do for so long, skim her fingers through his dark hair and along his hard jawbone. From the moment he'd placed his lips on hers, his dark eyes hot with promise, she'd been breathless with unleashed longing and intense excitement. As long as she lived she'd never forget his fevered and hungry look, their first hot kiss, the wild excitement sparking between them making his rejection afterward all the more devastating. Damn him.

While her anger at Sean had stabbed like a hot poker in her heart, she'd watched him carefully last night. Despite his stillness, despite his stoic expression, she'd seen true regret in his eyes. After she'd accused him of treating her like a stranger, he hadn't made excuses. Instead quiet shock reflected in his eyes, as if he'd never considered the emotional consequences of his lies.

What he didn't know, couldn't know, was that he'd hurt her badly because she'd wanted more from him than a working partnership. While she couldn't recall Bill Myer, the man she had married, she'd carried expectations about marriage into her relationship with Sean. She'd looked upon him as a husband, wanting his touch. Needing his trust.

And he'd given her misery and heartache. So now all she had to do was stop thinking of him as her husband. Forget about her expectancy of intimacy. Move on with her investigation without the hindrance of emotional baggage.

She would adjust. Adapt. Ignore the loss that had peeled away her protective shell and left her nerves raw. Showering and dressing quietly, she took her gun from under her pillow and holstered the weapon at her ankle. A hike up the mountain would help rid her of plaguing tension and let her face her situation from a new perspective.

Hoping the murder scene might provide a clue she'd overlooked before, she unlocked the bedroom door, still carrying her shoes so she wouldn't wake Sean, who slept on the couch, his back to her. Barely daring to breathe for fear of waking him, she slipped on her boots, donned her jacket and slipped out the door.

The sun's rays hadn't yet cleared the mountain, but the night sky was lightening to a gray dawn. She shivered, tugged on her gloves and tucked in the ends of her scarf. Refusing to let a few stray snowflakes deter her, she headed up the trail.

Snow crunched under her boots and the brisk pace she set kept her warm. Guilt pricked her that she hadn't left Sean a note, but she'd needed to be alone with her thoughts. Breathing in the cool air helped chase away the cobwebs left over from her sleepless night.

A half hour later, she passed the steep incline where Sean had saved her from slipping over the edge. She'd been looking down at her feet to maintain her footing on the icy trail, but when she reached a relatively flat spot, she checked the sky. Swirling wet snow blew horizontally across the mountain, engulfing her in an eerie silence of big white flakes.

Going back to Sean's cabin might be wise. Between her and Kesky lay miles of trackless hills choked with bushy ravines and rolling, hummock-dotted slopes. And the uphill walk to the mine was steeper than she'd recalled.

Spying an overhang where she could get out of the weather, Carlie took a breather. The wind had picked up. Going on up to the Dog Mush no longer seemed such a good idea. While she didn't think she would lose her way, the chilling wind and snow began to take a toll.

While she stopped to rest, her body heat cooled. Just about to turn back, Carlie heard a gunshot. Automatically, she dropped to the snow and pulled her gun from the ankle holster. Realizing her navy jacket made an ideal target against a while background, she crawled on elbows and knees toward a boulder.

Snow beneath her trembled. For a moment she feared she might be on a huge slab of snow that might break away from the side of the mountain and carry her to her death below.

Amid an eerie stillness, she raised her head and peered into the distance where she thought the shot had been fired from. But in the swirling storm, she couldn't see much but trees and mountain and snow.

Two more shots fired, echoing across the mountain.

Carlie inched behind the boulder, unsure whether anyone was even shooting at her. The shots hadn't kicked up any nearby snow. For all she knew, someone was hunting two miles away. But she refused to take chances.

At a strange rumbling overhead, she tilted her head back. The next moment the ground jerked out from under her. Clouds of snow whipped in the air. Earthquake? No, avalanche! She rolled, sliding with the loose snow.

From out of nowhere, Sean appeared, running an awkward zigzag pattern with the grace of a mountain cat over the uneven terrain. "Get up."

If she stood, she'd make an even better target. Her instinct was to stay low and crawl as fast as she could, aiming her weapon, ready to fire. "Someone's shooting."

Sean grabbed her shoulders and yanked her to her feet. "Run."

"But—"

Another shot echoed. A roar filled her ears. Sean tugged her forward so hard, her feet barely touched the ground. Below, her boots, the snow shifted. The wind picked up. Above them the mountain cracked, the roar louder than thunder.

She glanced over her shoulder and a fear unlike any she'd ever known possessed her. Surging snow and ice hurtled down the mountain, growing, tumbling, cascading over boulders, uprooting trees.

Alone, Sean might survive.

She screamed to be heard above the roar. "Go. Save yourself."

He squeezed her hand tighter. "Run."

She *was* running. Her lungs burst with the effort, her gun still clenched in her hand. Her thighs and calves screamed from the pressure she exerted.

Chunks of snow pelted her shoulders and slammed into her back. Rocks and roots and snow rolled beneath her feet. If not for Sean's strong grip on her hand, she would have fallen long ago.

She peeked up and gasped. They weren't going to make it. Sean was risking his life to save hers. Adrenaline surged through her, and she yanked her hand from his.

She shoved him forward. "Leave me."

"Carlie, no!"

She'd broken free of his grip. Her knees buckled. Without Sean to anchor her, she spun, pitching and rolling like a schooner caught in a waterspout. Snow flattened her. And all of a sudden, snow filled her eyes, crammed into her nose and mouth.

Darkness surrounded her.

Snow was under her, over her, to her right and left. She'd been buried alive. Dear God, she couldn't breathe. And the darkness mauled her.

Clawing with one hand, she struggled hard. The weight of the snow crushed her ribs. Her lungs burned. She wasn't sure which way was up.

She had to think.

Think.

Sean might be looking for her. She shouted, but

the snow muffled her voice. Darkness seared her with a rising panic.

Seconds passed. She had to think.

She didn't want to die on this frigid mountain where no one would find her until spring. Her fingers tightened reflexively.

She still had her gun.

If she discharged the weapon, Sean might hear her, pinpoint her location, dig her free. But she could shoot him by accident if she first didn't figure out which way was down.

Carlie brought her free hand to her face and cleared a few inches of snow, creating a hollow area around her hand and face. With her teeth, she pulled off her glove and let it fall, then felt around to see where it had landed, letting gravity tell her which direction was down.

With cold fingers she found the glove. As near as she could tell, up was somewhere over her left shoulder. She aimed the gun to her right and downward and pulled the trigger.

She counted to ten and fired again.

At the current rate, the eight bullets she had left would last little more than a minute. She wouldn't be conscious much longer than that.

Never doubting that Sean had beaten the odds and escaped the snow, she clung to the thought he would do everything in his power to dig her out of the dark, cold tomb.

Hang on.

She fired the seventh, or the eight bullet. Dizziness made her woozy.

"Carlie!"

Had someone shouted her name? Couldn't be sure. The effort of shouting back was too much. Too hard.

Still, she had to fire the gun. Gathering every last bit of remaining strength, she pulled the trigger one last time.

She had done all she could. The fight seeped out of her. Faces flashed before her. Her mother. Sister. A blond-haired man. Dark-haired man...

SEAN FRANTICALLY SCRATCHED through the snow where he lay half-buried. Just seconds ago, Carlie had pulled her hand from his, shoving him toward safety. Momentum had carried him to the edge of the avalanche chute and out of harm's way, to the side of a wide swath that looked as if cut by a mad cat-skinner and lined with broken trees. A mere instant had passed since the roaring snow had come to a halt and he'd seen Carlie disappear.

He stood upright, ignoring the snow on his face, the blood trickling from a cut on his lip. "Carlie?"

He spun left, right, and then again, searching for a sign of her golden hair, her blue parka. Damn it. She'd just been a few steps behind him. Where could she be buried?

He surveyed the mountainside he no longer recognized. Black cottonwood and balsam poplar and boulders had tumbled, carving new crevasses and paths. In places, he estimated the snow could be more than twenty feet deep. An icy chill settled between his shoulder blades at the thought of Carlie lying under all that snow. She would suffocate within minutes. He had to find her. Fast.

His rolling fall could have left them separated by

dozens of yards. Gauging from the spot he'd last seen her, guessing at where she might be, he dashed uphill and to the east. Even as he started to scoop snow with his hands, he suspected his effort would be futile.

Damn. Damn. Damn. She'd yanked her hand from his, imperiling her life to save his. Her courage and sacrifice fueled his digging. He didn't want to lose her. If she died, it would be his fault.

He'd lied to her and that had led to her coming out here alone. She must have been extra quiet leaving this morning, but he'd also been exhausted. He hadn't fallen asleep until the early hours of the morning or he'd have heard her leave. By the time he'd awakened, she was already long gone. He'd tracked her, almost catching up to her before the first shot sounded.

At first he'd thought the shooter had been aiming at Carlie. But the shooter took advantage of perfect avalanche conditions, trying to make an attempt on her life appear accidental. Whoever was after her was obviously afraid that she'd be able to identify Jackson's killer when her memory returned. And that person may have succeeded in keeping her quiet.

Forever.

Using his hands as a scoop, he stubbornly tossed the wet snow to one side.

Repeating the motion over and over without pausing for breath, he prayed he'd read the terrain correctly. There wasn't time for a second effort.

She could be anywhere.

"Carlie!"

He couldn't spare the breath to shout, yet he desperately needed an indication of her whereabouts.

"Carlie!"

Come on. Come on. Answer me.

A gun fired. Already deep in the hole he'd dug and protected by the snow, Sean barely paused. Whoever had started the avalanche with gunfire hadn't given up.

But neither would he. Not until Carlie was safe in his arms.

Ten seconds later another shot fired, oddly muffled and coming from under him. Under him?

At the memory of Carlie's gun attached to her shapely ankle, Sean realized she was answering him in the only way she could.

"Carlie. If you can hear me, fire two quick shots."

Like a metronome, she continued to fire every ten seconds. She couldn't hear him, which meant she was deeper than he'd hoped. And farther to his right. Sean angled the tunnel he was digging, letting her shots guide him.

His chest heaved from his efforts. Sweat trickled down his brow and into his eyes. He counted the shots. She only had two, maybe three more left.

He had to find her fast. She wouldn't remain conscious much longer.

She fired another shot. And he still hadn't spotted her.

"Hang on, babe. I'm almost there."

The eighth bullet urged him on to superhuman effort. He had to find her now.

The space he'd hollowed out was so deep, he had trouble throwing the snow high enough to clear the hole. The deeper he dug, the harder and more compacted the snow. Even if she'd found a tiny air pocket, no one could last down here for much longer than thirty minutes. More likely, she had less than four or five. If he'd guessed wrong on where to dig, his mistake would be her death sentence.

Through the white, he spied darkness. His pulse accelerated with hope. Using his hands as a shovel, he clawed away snow.

Her boot!

There was no time for gentleness. No time to figure out how she'd landed. No time to figure out the best way to extract her. He grabbed her ankle and tugged with all his strength.

Suction fought him. Sean wasn't about to let the snow keep her now. She tumbled into his lap, her fingers clenched in a death grip around the gun.

Wrenching off his gloves, Sean felt for her pulse at her neck. Her heart still beat strongly. Her face was pale, her lips had a bluish tinge.

He checked her breathing. Couldn't find signs that her lungs still worked. How long had she been deprived of oxygen? He had been too frantic to find her to stop and check his watch.

He had no idea how much time had passed.

Without room in the cramped hole to lay her on her back and breathe into her mouth, he simply pressed his mouth over hers, held her nose shut and prayed that the air he blew into her would start her own body working again.

"Come on. Breathe. Breathe."

A shudder hunched her shoulders.

"That's right, breathe."

She coughed weakly. And her eyelids fluttered open.

He'd never been so happy to see anyone in his life. "Welcome back."

"Knew...you'd...save me."

He smoothed the hair from her face. Color was returning. Her pink lips had lost the tinge of blue and her cheeks had regained some of their normal glow. She'd lost her hat and he removed his and placed it on her head. "You led me right to you by firing your gun."

"Didn't...shoot you?"

She had been worried about shooting him—while she was buried alive. What a woman. She'd kept her head, hadn't panicked in a situation where even the most experienced mountain man might have.

Tenderly he drew her head against his shoulder. "You were smart and very brave."

She tilted her head back, her eyes stark with unpleasant memories. "I didn't like the dark and I was scared." She shivered. "Scared and so cold."

He dipped his head until his mouth was just an inch from hers. "Let me warm you up."

She lifted her lips to his and he didn't hesitate another moment. He could have lost her before he'd really gotten to know her. His heart lifted at another chance. He intended to make the most of it.

Sean took his time, liking the feel of her on his lap, savoring the sleek taste of her. She was so feminine, yet solid. Softly muscled on the outside, but with nerves of steel on the inside. Stubborn as a glacier, with a heart of twenty-four-karat gold. Overly emotional, perhaps, but she was the kind of woman a man could count on. The kind of woman who was as strong as he was himself.

It gave him a strange feeling to think of her as his equal, to think that was what he wanted in a woman. Her frothing feminine confidence all but riveted his senses. He couldn't get enough of her. He wanted to taste her all over. He wanted her skin to skin. He wanted to hold her forever and never let her go. Ever.

She pulled back from their kiss first, studying him intently. "You said this wasn't a good idea."

"That was when I was trying to resist you."

Her eyebrow rose. "And now?"

"Now I find you irresistible." He leaned forward to kiss her again.

A light breeze swirled snowflakes around them. She placed a hand on his shoulder. "I want to go home, Sean. I've had enough snow and ice and darkness to last a lifetime."

With a shattered feeling, he surmised the rest of what she would say but had to hear the words. "And?"

"Your home is here in this wilderness." She rose to her feet and so did he. They stood so close in the confined space, touching at thighs, hips and chest. "You belong here. And I don't."

With a guarded expression, she was telling him she wasn't interested in pursuing anything more between them, telling him that sizzling passion wasn't enough to keep her here. He remained silent. He couldn't blame her.

He thought of the laser light focused on her head, the wire strung across the path, the avalanche created to bury her, of the danger she'd already faced because he'd insisted on keeping her with him. Her life had been in danger from the moment she'd arrived and he couldn't protect her. He'd been a fool to think he could. He should get her the hell away from Kesky before he was responsible for her death.

Shoving his disappointment and his sudden emptiness to the back of his mind, he forced himself to concentrate on their current predicament. First they had to climb out of the hole. Then he would take her home.

Soon he would have to say goodbye. A knot twisted in his abdomen. For her sake, he would find the strength to let her go.

Chapter Nine

Sean cupped his hands together and boosted Carlie out of the hole. Heart still racing from his megawatt kiss, fearful the shooter would spot her before she could take cover, she scrambled over the lip, wishing she had more ammunition to reload her gun. Helping Sean climb out while a shooter pinned them wouldn't be easy, but luckily, whoever had set off the avalanche seemed to have gone back into hiding.

Carlie appraised the seemingly empty mountain, where clouds concealed the peak and fog hid the lower portions, and bit her bottom lip worriedly. "How are you going to climb out?"

For an answer, Sean wedged his back and shoulders against one wall and propped his boots against the other. Slowly he worked his way up about three feet before the snow softened and collapsed. Like a cat, he landed on his feet.

"Thought that might happen."

"Maybe I should come back down and boost you out. Then you could pull me up," she suggested, wondering if she could make herself drop back into that freezing hole.

"The snow on the lip is too soft to hold both our weights." At Sean's refusal of her offer of help, she released a pent-up sigh of relief. While she still trembled from her ordeal, he appeared blasé about his predicament. "I'll just have to do this the hard way."

The hard way meant compacting snow and building steps solid enough to support his weight and climb to the next level. As unconcerned as if he were building a snowman, he worked at a methodical pace.

On the other hand, she couldn't stop shaking. Willow branches clicked overhead as if mocking her for escaping an early grave. If Sean hadn't estimated her location so precisely, her gunshots wouldn't have led him to her. As she surveyed the flat, desolate area between two steep ridges, she realized how lucky she'd been. Without Sean to dig her out, she would have suffocated. No one would have found her until spring.

She'd originally wanted to stay in Kesky and resolve Jackson's murder. But solving the case had turned deadly difficult with someone trying to stop her. If she remained, she might not live long enough to regain her memory. Better to recuperate elsewhere, even if in a jail cell. Sean hadn't said one word to try to stop her from leaving, a clear indication how little she meant to him. Sadness at what they might have had together filled her. Crossing her arms over her chest, she hugged herself. Jail might be lonely, but at least jail would be warm.

While Sean built his staircase, she glanced at the sky. Dark with the promise of more snow, cumulus clouds billowed, encompassing the mountaintop. The wind had let up as if gathering strength before a final assault, and she couldn't stop shivering.

Sean cleared the lip and pulled himself beside her, his dark eyes assessing her with concern. "We need to get you dry and warm as soon as possible. Can you walk about a quarter mile?"

His cabin was much farther than that, but she nodded and stood shakily, surprised her knees were so weak. She told herself that lack of oxygen had done a number on her, but more likely, his businesslike attitude after that scorching kiss had frayed her nerves ragged.

Without a word, Sean placed his arm around her waist to support her. "We'll take it nice and easy. A front just pushed back our storm. She won't hit for hours yet."

When Sean led her down a different path from the one she'd come up, she stopped, puzzled. "Where are we going?"

He tugged her onward. "Remember Wayne Riker, the mine's quartermaster who you met in town? Although he's not one of my favorite people, he has a cabin about a quarter mile east of here."

She nodded in agreement, pleased his first concern was her safety. As much as he disliked his quartermaster, his priority of getting her warm was more important than avoiding a man he disliked.

Fearful of another avalanche, she couldn't stop herself from glancing upward. Rocks and ice and fog did little to make her feel safer. A speck of neon green, careering down the mountain, caught her eye.

"Is that Tyler?"

"None other."

"How'd he get to the mountaintop?" she asked, thinking his location suspicious. Tyler seemed to be safely above the avalanche line, and she wondered if he could have been the shooter.

"Sometimes one of the miners takes him up on a snowmobile. Other times he parachutes out of an airplane."

"That's insane."

Sean hugged her close. "You have to be crazy to like extreme skiing."

"Crazy enough to start an avalanche?" she asked, curious to see what Sean thought of her sudden suspicions of Tyler. The kid had a knack for showing up just after someone had attempted to kill them. But then he spent the majority of his free time on the mountain.

"Why would he want to start an avalanche?" Sean asked patiently.

"To get rid of me before my memory returns. But I can't think of a motive for him to have killed Jackson."

Walking downhill to Wayne's cabin was much easier than the upward trek from Sean's place. Between Sean's supporting arm at her waist and the exercise, her blood heated, her stomach settled.

Ten minutes later, they rounded a bend. In a clearing below them stood a small cabin, its back quarter buried by an avalanche of snow. Under scudding clouds, dark, angry smoke swirled from the chimney. Hellish sparks shot into the gray sky, and in the distance, a wolf keened.

Sean slowed his footsteps. "Looks like Wayne's

home got hit by an offshoot of the avalanche that caught us. And he has company. See the tracks.''

He pointed to footprints in the snow that led back to Kesky. Like a wolf guarding its territory, Sean raised his head and sniffed the air. ''Do you smell gasoline?''

''I'm not sure.'' Her stomach churned and again she wished for bullets for her empty gun. She didn't relish walking onto another avalanche site and glanced uneasily at the cabin's setting. ''Maybe this isn't a good idea. We could go to your cabin instead.''

''You need to get warm.'' Sean finished his inspection of the cabin. ''And there's a good fire roaring down there judging from the density of those sparks.''

''I don't like the way that cabin looks.''

Sean didn't make fun of her premonition. Instead he tried to reason with her. ''Maybe Wayne got caught in the snow and needed to warm up fast, too. Or perhaps a trapper is waiting out the storm.''

He didn't sound convinced of his own words. And although her wilderness instincts couldn't match Sean's, she knew something was very wrong in that cabin half-buried by snow. She could feel it.

Sean unwrapped his arm from around her waist. ''Stay here while I check out the situation.''

''But—''

''I'll be back soon.'' He walked away, silent as a shadow, making himself one with the mountain.

Immediately, she missed his presence. She'd come to rely on not just his physical strength but his emotional support. For a man who preferred to live alone, he often had a way of making her feel as if she was part of a team. So when he abandoned her without a backward look, he took her by surprise.

She didn't like him leaving her out of the decision-making process. She didn't like being left alone. And she sure as hell didn't like letting him walk into a dangerous situation while she huddled in relative safety.

Restraining her impulse to follow, she debated with herself. Sean didn't have a weapon. He could be walking straight into a trap.

And yet, she might be a hindrance if she followed, unintentionally giving away their location. Sometimes he worked with her, but Sean could just as easily take charge without giving her a chance to question him. He'd frequently evaluated the problem and come to a decision before she'd even thought up the right questions. Normally fast on the uptake, Carlie knew coping in the wilds of Alaska was far from her forte. So she deferred to Sean's greater knowledge and waited, but she didn't have to like it.

Behind a pile of boulders and out of sight of the cabin, she paced to keep away the chill while keeping an eye on Sean's progress. He covered a lot of ground quickly with amazing stealth, and she realized how much she'd impeded his speed. She recalled his patience. Not once had he complained about her slowing his pace. Not once had he castigated her for heading up the mountain alone and almost getting both of them killed.

The man had his good points. He was an awesome kisser. Instinct told her he'd be a giving and passionate lover. Common sense told her not to let herself become any more fascinated with him than she already was. Sean McCabe was a loner who would feel caged in a city, while she couldn't wait to leave the cold, menacing mountains.

He wasn't the man for her. They didn't even have common interests. Sean's idea of fun was a twenty-mile hike through frozen mountains. Hers was a day doing no more than baking on a sizzling sand beach. She liked movies and restaurants and couldn't imagine daily life without a telephone. Or her family. Or specialty chocolate. Sean was an entity unto himself, requiring little, content with himself and his mountain.

And yet she couldn't deny how attractive she found the intense way he looked at her when he didn't think she was watching. As if he was memorizing her every movement. She liked the aroma of cedar that clung to his skin, his eyes flaring hotly before he kissed her. And she liked the way his kiss turned her knees to molten metal.

But she didn't care for the way he closed himself off from her, giving the barest answers to questions he considered too personal. She wondered if after she returned to Florida, she would regret that they hadn't made love.

"Hey, Carlie!" Sean waved his arms at her, gesturing her to follow him. "It's all right."

Whoever he'd found inside the cabin, he didn't consider a threat. Putting aside her daydreams, she hurried down, glad her reflections about what could have been between them would fade long before she caught up with him.

Sean waited until she joined him and ushered her

through the front door. The cabin had been ransacked. Every drawer was open. Clothing, supplies and papers lay scattered. Dishes, cups and utensils spilled across the kitchen floor, a pan of sourdough starter trampled. Mastodon tusks and old walrus and mammoth ivory lay scattered along with a collection of geodes, flints and soapstone inside a smashed cabinet. Animal heads, stuffed and mounted on the walls, stared down at Carlie and she shuddered in distaste.

At the sound of a man clearing his throat, she jumped. "Who's here?"

"It's me." Marvin strode out of the back room, a frown on his face.

The gambler's presence all the way up here struck her as odd. First, it was daytime, and the man had explained how he slept away the daylight hours. And like the banker, Ian Finley, she'd bet Marvin rarely left town.

Despite the heat seeping past her jacket, she couldn't seem to get warm. Although Sean didn't think the man posed a threat and as much as she respected his judgment, Carlie was more suspicious. Half-expecting Marvin to pull a gun and order them to put their hands up, she eased out of her wet jacket, thinking it odd that every window was wide open and letting in the cold air and an occasional snowflake.

Besides her, Sean didn't relax, but neither did he tense, indicating he probably already knew Marvin was there. Still, Sean eclipsed the space he occupied, taking control with a subtle mastery that wouldn't have left a stranger in any doubt he was in charge.

Gold tooth glinting, Marvin gestured to the open window. "The gas fumes are about gone. We can shut the windows now."

"Was the wood wet? Did you pour the gas to start the fire?" Sean asked.

Marvin spit tobacco juice out a window then shook his head. "The only thing I've touched is the windows."

While the men closed other windows, Carlie unwrapped her wet scarf and removed her gloves, placing her hands near the fire for warmth.

"What brings you here?" she asked Marvin.

The gambler spoke to her with his hands outstretched and away from his body, as if he knew that she still suspected him of Jackson's murder or of carrying a weapon. "I have bad news."

Sean shut the last window and shot Marvin a long look. "Carlie's had a rough morning. She needs to get dry and warm." Sean headed for a doorway, which she assumed led to a bedroom. "I'll see what I can find—"

"Don't go in there," Marvin said, his tone more a warning than an order.

Bits of snow melted in Carlie's hair and dripped down her neck. As much as she would have liked a dry robe or towel, she feared that if Sean stepped over the threshold, he might be heading into danger. Sean stopped and looked at Marvin.

The gambler was assessing her. "You look as if you've been making snow angels."

Sean glanced into the back room and then stared hard at Marvin. "Are you armed?"

Marvin frowned, his gaze glancing from Sean to Carlie and back. "Should I be?"

Sean let the question dangle in the air unanswered for a moment before breaking the tense silence. "Gunshots set off an avalanche. Carlie got caught in it."

His brief summary, so typical of his nature, didn't mention his role in saving her life, didn't give one more speck of information than was absolutely necessary. He would make a good cop, a good partner.

Marvin crossed his arms over his chest, his eyes staring out the window. "She survived. Wayne wasn't so lucky." He paused and then locked gazes with Sean. "And no, I'm not armed. But maybe after what happened in there—" he nodded toward the back room "—I should start carrying a weapon."

Carlie's neck prickled. "What's happened?"

"Wayne's dead. The avalanche caught him standing by the back room's window." Marvin rubbed his chin. "I would have thought it an accident, but look at this place. Someone came in, searching for something, and tried to burn the place with gasoline. Only I interrupted him."

Or maybe Marvin was the killer, and they'd caught him before he could hide the evidence of his crime. Stunned by the news of a second suspicious death, Carlie didn't know what to think. Marvin was one of her primary suspects in Jackson's murder, and now he'd shown up at a second death scene.

Carlie raised an eyebrow. "Why did you come up here?"

Marvin squared his shoulders. "Wayne lost some

money last night during our poker game. He said he'd reimburse me this morning.''

Something about Marvin's attitude bothered her, but she couldn't quite put her finger on it. On the outside, he was one cool customer. Inside him, she sensed cunning intelligence he didn't quite let show.

Hoping to provoke him into a possible mistake, Carlie let suspicion enter her tone. ''And you climbed all the way up the mountain to get paid?''

''Look, I know you suspect me of killing Jackson. And now Wayne. But I didn't do it.'' Marvin shuddered. ''I'm not the violent type. Besides, I'm not the one with a grudge against Wayne.''

Carlie shoved to her feet. ''What do you mean?''

''Wayne didn't get along with many of the mountain men who grew up in the area,'' Marvin explained.

''Why not?''

''He hunted for sport,'' Sean answered, heading toward the bedroom. Almost warm, Carlie followed, curious to investigate another death and see if she could find any similarities with Jackson's murder.

Marvin paled. ''Sean, don't let her go back there. Death isn't a pretty sight.''

She brushed by Sean, pleased when he didn't try to stop her. ''I'm a cop, remember?''

Snow had poured through the open door, surged through a broken window and invaded the house, demolishing a spruce-pole bunk. Belly-up, Wayne Riker lay buried to his waist in a pile of snow, eyes wide open, his rifle across his chest, no sign of his walking stick in sight. Terror had frozen his facial muscles into a ghastly mask.

Carlie leaned over the shotgun and sniffed. "It's been fired recently." She touched the body, which still held the last traces of heat. He couldn't have been dead long. She glanced at Sean, who stood in the middle of the room, touching nothing, but she suspected he would remember every detail.

While Sean remained still, she searched for evidence that would suggest Wayne Riker had died from anything other than natural causes. She wasn't a forensic expert, but she didn't think his body had been moved. His neck cocked sideways at an unnatural angle, indicating that the snow had knocked him to the side, the fall snapping his neck.

Carlie tried to consider the angles of trajectory but had difficulty keeping all the perspectives of the mountain in her head. "Could Wayne have fired at us through the back window, set off the avalanche and been caught in his own trap?"

"It's possible." Sean studied the snow, and she could almost hear gears shifting in his brain as he considered the possibilities. "More likely he was out hunting."

"Yoo-hoo!" A youthful voice shouted from the living area.

Carlie straightened. "Tyler?"

"He's not one who likes to miss any excitement." Sean opened a closet, pulled out several towels and a thick robe and handed them to Carlie. "You need to change into dry clothes."

In the other room, she overheard Marvin filling in Tyler on Wayne's death. The kid sounded shocked, but faking surprise wouldn't be all that hard to do.

And the kid's ski tracks were all over the mountain—which proved zip.

Carlie ignored the robe and accepted the towels. She covered her shoulders with one cloth and wrapped her hair in the other. "I'm okay. It's mostly my hair that's wet."

Drying her hair as best she could, she followed Sean back to the main room. Tyler thumped across the floor in his ski boots, his cheeks pink with excitement. "Did you see that avalanche?"

"Know how it started?" Sean asked.

For the moment, Carlie was content to dry her hair and let Sean ask the questions. But she carefully watched Marvin's and Tyler's faces as Sean spoke.

Marvin hunkered down by the fire, a grimace on his lips. "I heard gunshots."

Tyler unzipped his ski jacket. "I didn't."

"Maybe you were up too high," Carlie suggested, wishing Tyler would remove his tinted ski goggles so she could get a better look into his eyes. "We heard gunshots, too."

Sean faced the skier, his tone casual but his eyes bright with a trace of curiosity. "Who brought you up the mountain today?"

"Roger." Tyler flung himself over the arm of the couch, nervously twisting one of his gold earrings. "He said he had some thinking to do."

Carlie rubbed her hair with the towel, again wondering if this death could be connected to Jackson's. "Did Roger have a weapon with him?"

"He never goes anywhere without his rifle," Marvin muttered crossly. "I'm the only damned fool who walks around unarmed."

Carlie surveyed Tyler's jacket, which boasted pockets in the sleeves as well as the usual places. He had more than ample space to hide a gun on him. "You ski with a·gun?"

Tyler shrugged as if in apology. "There're bears in these mountains. I read somewhere that a person is statistically more likely to be killed by a bear in Alaska than run over by a taxi in New York City."

Great.

Once again there was a suspicious death—which might be an accident. But something about the angle of the neck injury bothered her, niggled at her memory. But she couldn't quite remember.

And once again Tyler, Roger and Marvin had been close by. Any of the three of them could have fired the shots into the loose snow, setting off the avalanche. While Marvin claimed to be unarmed, he could have stashed a gun somewhere.

Or Wayne could have set off the avalanche himself.

Just great. She had nothing to go on.

"Maybe Wayne's death is an accident," Tyler suggested, seemingly oblivious to the mess in the cabin around him.

Marvin rubbed his jaw thoughtfully. "Wayne's neck looked broken."

Tyler loosened the ankle attachments of his boots. "Maybe his neck snapped when the snow knocked him down."

Or maybe a killer knew the exact spot to strike. Was the murderer skilled in hand-to-hand combat? An ex-marine? The possibilities were endless.

"Did Wayne have any enemies?" Carlie asked.

"He kept to himself a lot. I didn't like him," Marvin admitted.

"Me, neither," Sean added.

"But he worked for you."

"He did his job well."

Carlie wasn't surprised that Sean would overlook his dislike of a man and keep him on the payroll. Good at bottling up his feelings and keeping his emotions at bay, he let his practical side rule his decision-making processes.

"You guys sound like you're detectives in an old *Colombo* rerun. I still think it was an accident," Tyler said again.

Marvin shook his head. "You're wrong. Someone went through Wayne's things, maybe tried to burn down the cabin to hide the evidence."

Tyler rolled his eyes. "What evidence?"

"Maybe something's missing," Carlie suggested. "What did Wayne own of value?"

Sean sat beside her on the couch, took her hand and squeezed. "He owned stock in the mine."

Hoping the others didn't notice, she lightly squeezed back. Just having those hard calluses and strong fingers touching her lent a certain strength to her thoughts.

This was the first time Sean had touched her, not out of lust, not to physically help her over some difficulty, but to give comfort. She thought it significant and sad how he'd reached out to her *after* she'd told him she wanted to go home. Her imminent departure meant he was safe from her. Safe to retreat behind the lonely existence he'd built for himself. A ragged pain sliced through her heart at how much hurt the boy he'd been must have endured to grow into the man sitting so still beside her. Didn't he realize that he'd built the walls around himself so high that no one could get in?

She'd tried to be patient, tried to give him time to realize she wasn't a threat to him. But his past had left scars. He still hadn't told her much about his childhood. Most likely, he never would. Although he'd seemed unable to resist kissing her, he resisted being swept away by emotions. Even lust. She didn't dare hope he would ever let himself feel anything more, and she needed to put some distance between them before she came to care for him any more than she already did.

Stop daydreaming. Stop thinking about him. She forced herself to pick up the thread of the conversation.

Tyler's impatient tone helped draw her from her thoughts. "But the gold Wayne hid here would be a much more desirable target." Tyler took off his hat and shook out his hair. "Wayne didn't like paper money. Didn't trust banks. He took his pay in gold dust and buried it."

Sean pinned Tyler with a stare. "How do you know he buried his gold?"

"He mentioned it one night after he'd drunk too much." Tyler shrugged. "He never said where. I guess come spring we could probe around with a metal detector and see what turns up."

Carlie kept hold of Sean's hand, appreciating his warmth, however bittersweet. "I can't see someone killing Wayne for his gold and waiting until spring to find it. We're missing something. We just don't have all the pieces yet."

Chapter Ten

Eager to fly Carlie to safety, first Sean directed her into the Yellow Submarine, Ian Finley's bank, the next morning. Sean figured he owed his new business partner an explanation for his upcoming out-of-town trip.

However, he had no intention of speaking to Ian about the three attempts on Carlie's life. Or that someone else in Kesky was Jackson's murderer. The less Sean said, the less chance there would be of the murderer hearing of his plans and the safer Carlie would be.

His business would survive an overnight trip to Fairbanks.

The weather had finally broken, and although the phone lines into Kesky were still down, Ian could either reopen the mine if the weather warmed and if he wanted to supervise production or wait until Sean returned. Most likely, the weather had closed them for the winter.

Sean and Carlie walked up to the teller window. Tyler greeted them with a pleasant smile. "What can I do for you?"

"I want to cash a check, please." Sean slipped the piece of paper under the plastic window.

Tyler glanced at the check, turned to his money drawer, then looked at the check again and frowned. "I don't have that much cash in my drawer. Hold on and I'll find Mr. Finley. Would you care for a cup of coffee?" He gestured to a coffeepot and foam cups along the wall. "I'll just be a minute."

Sean poured them coffee while Carlie perused a discolored map of the area that hung on the wall. "It looks ancient."

"Nothing much has changed around here in the last fifty years."

"No kidding."

"We're not on the Marine Highway, and the Alaskan Highway runs from Dawson Creek to Fairbanks but never made it out this way. Since Kesky is far from the regular tourist routes, we haven't been invaded by the lower forty-eight."

The corners of Carlie's mouth twitched upward. "I don't think you have to worry."

She didn't even pretend to like the quaintness of the town—not that he could blame her after the experience she'd had here. Still, as he sipped hot coffee and watched her look at the map, he realized how desirable she looked in her hooded parka. Her eyes sparkled like sunlit emeralds, her hair glimmered with a golden sheen and her full lips looked utterly kissable.

Just thinking about kissing her again made his blood surge. Damn it. He was taking her to Fairbanks. While her life was in danger, he couldn't keep her here just because he wanted to taste her lips again. Just because he ached to skim his fingers over her lightly tanned skin. Just because he wanted to bury his hands in her hair and breathe in her scent of sunshine.

What in blazes was taking Tyler so long?

Finishing the last of his coffee, Sean tossed the cup into the trash can. Carlie pointed to the mountain range that hemmed in Kesky to the east. "We have to fly over those to get to Fairbanks?"

"We don't have to clear the peaks. We'll fly through a pass." He traced their route with his finger.

She pointed to a blue spot high in the mountains. "Is that a lake?"

"In summer, it's the prettiest place you've ever seen. Trout run two-, two-and-a-half feet."

Tyler returned and put on his ski jacket. "Got to run an errand. Mr. Finley will be right out with your money, Sean." He waved at them and hurried out.

A door opened and Ian Finley exited his office, his bald head shiny under fluorescent lights, a thick envelope in his hand. "Sorry to keep you waiting. I had to open the safe."

Carlie frowned at Tyler's desertion but she remained silent, refilling her cup of coffee.

The banker handed the money to Sean, who counted it then placed it inside his front shirt pocket. "I'm not opening the mine for another day or two—"

Ian grimaced at him through his gold-rimmed glasses. "But the weather's clearing."

"Exactly. I'm flying to Fairbanks to pick up a few supplies. Should be back tomorrow."

Ian scratched his head. "I intended to be a silent

partner. But I can't say I like the idea of closing the Dog Mush for another forty-eight hours. Miners have to work. People in this town live paycheck to paycheck.''

"The men have been paid out of my pocket. We can work through the weekend if the weather holds. The ground's freezing fast. Most likely, with the weather this cold, we'll be shutting down for the winter within a week or two, anyway.''

"And if the weather turns, you might be socked in Fairbanks for days.''

Sean didn't appreciate the man questioning his decision but controlled his irritation by reminding himself Ian owned as much of the Dog Mush as he did. "You want to go up and work with a crew, that's fine by me.''

"You're leaving because of her—'' Ian jutted his chin at Carlie "—aren't you?''

Sean let an edge of hardness enter his tone. "That's my business.''

Carlie immediately felt his annoyance.

Ian didn't seem to notice. "You take her to Fairbanks, she could disappear. Jackson might never receive justice.''

Carlie swallowed, distaste pinching her lips as if the coffee had suddenly turned bitter. "I didn't kill him.''

"Then your memory has returned?'' Ian asked, his tone challenging her with a boldness Sean didn't care for.

"I'm afraid not.'' Carlie held the man's stare with a calm that made Sean proud. She was smart enough not to let Ian force her into making any admissions, strong enough to stand up to him without raising her voice or causing a fuss, and he regretted how little time they had left together.

Sure he found her looks tempting. What red-blooded man wouldn't? But her inner strength called to him, excited him on a sexual level. He wanted to tap into her strength, enflame her passions.

Intuitively, he knew she wouldn't pine away if a husband abandoned her like his mother had. Carlie Myer had a steel rod for a backbone that didn't detract one iota from her femininity.

Keeping himself from taking her to bed had been one of the hardest things he'd ever done. The pent-up sexual tension arching between them had him antsy as a teenager, but she wasn't a woman who would accept a fling and he couldn't offer her more. Long ago he'd accepted he was meant to live alone in the mountains where he belonged.

Despite a few lapses, he hadn't lost control. But for a moment, longing overwhelmed him and he imagined a life with this woman for a mate. She was a woman who could give him fiery daughters and spirited sons.

He thought of her reading to a daughter or son all cuddled on her lap. He thought of her making his house into a home. He thought of sharing the long, cold winters with her laughter to warm him. He couldn't imagine ever suffering from cabin fever with a woman like Carlie to share his life. He imagined waking up next to her in the morning, talking with her during the day, snuggling through endless nights filled with passion. At the ache in his chest, he shoved the pleasant thoughts away with ruthless precision. He already dreaded making the return trip to his cabin, which would be empty without her. No need to torture himself with what could never be.

Her voice softened as she soothed Ian. "I'm beginning to wonder if my memories will ever return."

Only slightly mollified, the banker stuck his hands in his pockets and turned toward his office. "Well, if you don't remember, you can't know for certain whether you killed him or not."

Sean took her arm and her eyes flashed him a grateful look. "Bye, Ian. Thanks for the coffee."

"DON'T WE HAVE TO FILE a flight plan?" Carlie settled into the co-pilot's seat of Sean's seaplane.

Sean flipped switches on a panel over his head, starting his preflight check. He'd already inspected the landing skis and had generally looked the plane over. Now inside, he tested the rudders to be sure nothing was jamming and tested the ailerons and flaps. He flashed her a rare grin. "Bush pilots fly by the seat of their pants. We don't have runways, airports or control towers."

While he performed his preflight check, Carlie looked out the window. He'd taken her downriver from Kesky. Here, the water widened into a calm rolling river with inch-high chop marring the surface. The peaceful beauty of her surroundings warred with her internal chafing to be gone. She looked over her shoulder back toward Kesky then silently chastised herself for the uneasiness. While several seaplanes lay along the bank tied down with lines to the trees on shore, they couldn't have been more alone. There was no one to help untie the plane. There was no dock.

Still, she would be glad once Sean flew the plane into the sky. She couldn't shake the feeling that someone in the trees was watching them, but after fruitlessly searching the shoreline, she gave up. Miles and miles of trees lined the river that ran a course as far as her eyes could see. From the banker's map she'd seen that the state was mostly empty with thousands of acres of forest and tundra, miles of rivers and streams, hidden valleys, coves, bays and mountains spread across an area so vast it staggered her imagination.

Sean threw her luggage in a rear compartment, topped off the fuel by siphoning gasoline from a barrel and helped her into the plane. While Carlie didn't have a fear of flying, she had doubts about her safety. The plane, smelling of fuel and stale sweat, sported assorted dents and clearly needed a paint job.

"When was the last time a mechanic checked out—"

"This baby may not look like much, but mechanically she's in top-notch shape."

Sean busied himself with his switches and gauges, then started the engine. The plane glided like a catamaran atop the water, skimming the surface with a smooth surge of power. Within a few short moments, Sean lined up the plane with the river. The engines roared and their speed increased.

Once they were airborne, Carlie relaxed her shoulders. Until now, she hadn't realized how tense she'd been. "I thought someone might try and stop us from leaving."

At the mention of her fears, Sean frowned. "It was almost too easy."

Her ears popped as they lifted higher into the air. "Maybe we're paranoid."

"And maybe not." Sean frowned again.

Her pulse skipped a beat. "Something wrong?"

"As we took off, I thought I just saw Roger along the river. He had his gun on his shoulder."

"How could you tell?"

"No one else in Kesky wears a bright yellow and black parka."

"Was he aiming at us?"

"I only caught a glimpse of him." Sean's sharp eyes checked and rechecked his gauges. "We seem fine. Relax. I'm not flying any white-knuckle special," he teased. "Why don't you sit back and enjoy the view."

She gave him a smile, knowing it to be weak, and settled into her seat. "Are you trying to distract me?"

"What do you think?" His smile was slow and sinfully sexy.

She bit the inside of her lip. Although she ached to respond to his playfulness, regret filled her and she did as he'd suggested, studying the view.

Before them a snow-capped mountain range rose majestically out of the fogged-in earth. She couldn't help being impressed by the immense area that showed no signs of humanity. Oddly that was a comfort.

High up in the mountains, she saw waterfalls frozen in splendor and, wherever she looked, endless forests of evergreens. Huge outcroppings of granite and snow-dusted pines towered inspiringly into the thin air. It all seemed wild and untamed to her southern eyes, accustomed to long, flat vistas studded with palms and sandy beaches.

She understood why Sean loved this state. The awesome mountains lent a timeless feel while retaining a sense of adventure. A man or woman could feel free here, free to throw off the past and make a brand-new start in a thriving frontier.

Sean must have caught a glimpse of her breathless wonder. "Like the view?"

"It's awesome."

"One out of five men in Alaska are pilots. The tourist brochures say that's because our cities have no other way in or out. But they're wrong."

"Really?"

"We fly for the same reason we like to look at women—to appreciate the beauty."

He was no longer talking about the view, but about her. At his compliment, a warm glow filled her which she tried to ignore. In two hours, he'd drop her off in Fairbanks and they'd never see each other again. She subdued her feelings of regret. Leaving Kesky and Sean was what she wanted.

Admiration turned his voice husky. "You're as strong as those mountains, Carlie. You're a survivor."

More compliments. She wanted to look at him and say thanks with a casual boldness, but she couldn't force the words past the lump in her throat. Just like the crazy Alaskan weather, Sean had a way of throwing surprises at her. Why did he have to be so nice to her now that she was leaving? Didn't he realize their parting would be easier if he returned to the gruff, hard man he'd been when they'd met?

A squirrelly gust hit the plane, diverting Sean's attention. The engines went silent. They didn't sputter or choke or cough. One moment they were roaring merrily away, the next they simply stopped.

Terror churned her stomach. "Are we out of fuel?"

"No. Don't worry, I'll restart the engine." Sean flipped switches, his eyes sharp with concentration.

Nothing happened.

Air whistled over the windshield and whipped around the edges. She expected the plane to take a dive. But Sean held her level.

"We can glide down. Put your parka back on."

She stared at the rocky face of the mountain in front of them. Sheer cliffs, steep ridges and rock faces dominated her view. They wouldn't clear the mountain peak and there was no place to land. She couldn't spot one flat area in ten miles. But she did as she was told, donning her jacket and then buckling up.

"How long do we have?"

"Long enough to make Sunrise Lake, I hope."

"You hope?"

"We're losing altitude faster than I'd like."

"Can we dump fuel?"

"This isn't a commercial airliner."

They were about to make a forced landing in the middle of nowhere. Even if they survived the crash, she estimated their chances of survival at zip. No one would know they were missing for at least several days. No one would even come looking for them.

Her family would never know what had happened to her.

In the window, the mountain grew larger, filling the entire view.

"Hold on," Sean yelled, banking the plane around the face of the mountain.

Her stomach heaved with the sickening swoop of the plane. Up ahead, she spotted a flat, snow-covered area. Sunrise Lake. But it looked frozen.

Sean spoke in clipped sentences. "This plane isn't meant to land on hard surfaces. The ice may not hold our weight. The waterskis may dig into the snow and ice. We could flip."

She gulped, knowing she'd never been so close to looking at death in the face, yet confident that Sean would try to keep them safe. "What should I do?"

"Get out of the plane as soon as we're down. The fuel can explode or we could sink."

They could burn. Or drown. Or freeze. Some choices. With terrifying speed the lake rose up below them.

"Behind your seat is a first aid kit and a survival pack. Grab them and get out of the plane."

"What about you?"

"I'll be right behind you."

Carlie wanted to close her eyes but couldn't. They were about to make a forced landing. His face tight with concentration, Sean fought the plane and the wind, keeping the wings level in the eerie silence.

"Remember, once we're down—"

"Get out fast."

Surveying the snow-covered ice under them, Carlie held her breath. She'd expected the frozen lake to be flat with no obstructions. But winds had piled the snow into uneven drifts.

While she looked out the window in horror, the plane lost altitude quickly. One moment they were in the air, the next grinding and crunching onto the ice. The plane's skis, meant for landing on water, tore through the snow, struck hard on the ice.

The horrendous crack of metal tearing was followed by the plane tilting dangerously to Sean's side. A wing caught and ripped free. The plane slid across the ice on its side, sparks flickering in the air.

Snow built up in front of the sliding plane, barely slowing their momentum. Blood rushed to her head, the forces so great she couldn't turn her head to look at Sean.

The bitter odor of gasoline filled her nostrils and smoke seeped from somewhere, making it difficult to breathe. She must have blacked out, because she came to in icy water. Groggily, she realized the entire cockpit was full of water.

Still inside the airplane, she was swimming in icy water and had no chance to take a breath. In the murky water she couldn't see a thing. She couldn't tell if she was on her side, right side up or upside down. Her harness kept her pinned.

She reached for the buckle and almost panicked. She couldn't see Sean, couldn't find the supply bag. Her icy clothes weighted her down and she struggled, her hands going ninety miles an hour, feeling for the windshield, the side of the plane, the door latch.

She couldn't find the door. Tried to go out the windshield but couldn't find an opening big enough to go through. But suddenly she sensed a presence beside her. Sean.

He kicked out the windshield. Water rushed and swirled.

She had no idea how much time had elapsed. She had to draw a breath—knew if she tried, she'd drown.

Something bumped her. The survival bag? She grabbed the strap, looping it over her shoulders to keep her hands free.

The water pressure changed. Sean grabbed her. She started gulping water. Moving her hands, kicking her feet became impossible. Her body went limp.

Choking and spitting, gasping for air, she opened her eyes on the surface. Somehow Sean had pulled her out of the water and onto the ice.

"You'll be okay now. Just rest."

He turned away from her.

"Where are you going?" she asked weakly, her body shaking so hard with the cold she could barely speak.

"Back to the plane. We need my emergency locator transmitter."

"No!" If he dived back into those icy waters she'd never see him again, she just knew it. She'd lose him like she'd lost Bill, and she couldn't bear to lose another man she loved. In one instant she realized she'd regained her memory, and in the next that she loved the man who'd just saved her life—as much as the man who'd made her a widow. Bill had been the man of a young girl's dreams. And Sean was the man for whom her woman's heart yearned. Carlie knew she'd been twice blessed. Determinedly, she strove to hang on to the man she would like to spend the rest of her life with. She knew Sean well enough to grasp that logic wouldn't dissuade him from reentering the icy water and risking his life. The plane was gone, sinking to the lake bottom.

She refused to lose another man she loved.

Desperate to keep him safe, she seized his ankle and pleaded with him. "Don't leave me. Please, I'm so cold."

Sean hesitated, kneeled and helped her up. He brushed her dripping hair out of her face. "I won't leave you."

"Promise?"

He nodded and took the bag from her shoulder. "You did well. We can survive with what's in here. Now we have to keep moving or we'll freeze."

Her heart lifted. She didn't even feel guilty for using his past against him. Instinctively, she'd known Sean wouldn't leave a woman in trouble. And if keeping him safe meant he thought her weak and needy, she didn't care—as long as he was safe.

With a creaking moan, the plane dipped below the lake's surface, a sickening plop echoing in her ears. Thank God Sean hadn't been inside the plane. If he'd disappeared beneath that icy lake with the airplane, her heart would have died with him.

He'd stayed and relief filled her. With this man at her side, she could do anything. Walk across a frozen lake, dripping wet, with a wind-chill factor way below zero.

They struggled to the lake's bank, wading through snowdrifts. Her hands and feet went from cold to icy to numb. He wouldn't let her stop, pushing her every time she slowed. The exhausting effort kept her blood flowing. But by the time they reached the lake's edge, she was having difficulty keeping her eyes open.

Sean shook her shoulders, his voice sharp with worry. "Don't go to sleep."

"Can't keep my eyes open." Even saying the words was an effort. She sagged to a sitting position.

Sean lifted her into his arms, cradling her like a baby. "Stay awake. Stay awake for me."

"I'll try."

Sean carried her from the lake into the woods. He had to be just as cold as she was, just as tired, but he seemed to thrive on the hardship. His determination to keep her safe glowed from his eyes like that of a man on a holy mission.

She couldn't let him down. She had to stay awake.

"My memory came back, Sean," she rambled, her cheek pressed against his icy parka. "I remember Bill. I loved him so much. He was a good man. A fine husband."

"He was my friend."

"Your best friend. I think he would like us being together. He'd tell you so if he could."

Sean's breath floated out of his mouth in harsh white puffs. "Do you remember who killed Jackson?"

"Who?"

Her thoughts floated away on a cloud. She closed her eyes, but instead of darkness she saw a tunnel of light. Bill was at the end of the tunnel, his face serene, his eyes calm, holding out his arms to her with a welcoming and gentle smile full of love.

She floated toward him.

Chapter Eleven

Sean set Carlie on the snowy floor inside a small cave he'd found in the lee of the gnawing wind. He didn't have much time. If her body temperature dropped too far, she wouldn't recover. Time and cold were his enemies now.

During the crash, he'd smashed his head against something. Blood from a cut in his mouth slid down his throat. His ankle was swollen and stiff and he'd gritted his teeth as he'd carried Carlie from the lake. Putting her down wasn't an option. They would survive together or die together.

And he refused to let her die. Finding the cave had been only the first step to keeping her alive. His hands shook terribly as he fumbled with the watertight bag Carlie had rescued in the crash. If he didn't get her dry and warm soon, she wouldn't last until morning. Her lips had already turned a deep blue. Her hair had frozen into stiff icicles.

Dumping the bag's contents out onto the snow, he retrieved a plastic tarp, a sleeping bag and extra pairs of woolen socks. Ignoring the emergency supplies of lighter, pot, tin cups, flares and dried food, he spread the tarp over the snow and then opened the sleeping bag.

After removing her weapon from her ankle and stripping Carlie of every stitch of wet clothing, he put the spare socks on her feet and over her hands as mittens and lifted her onto the sleeping bag. He removed his own clothes and joined her, using what little remaining body heat he had to warm her. Her skin, frosty as a snowman's, arrowed fear straight to his gut. She was so cold. Too cold.

He rubbed her skin briskly to increase her circulation. Hypothermia was his first concern. Frostbite the second.

A few minutes later, she opened her eyes. "Sean?"

"You'll be fine. Can you move your fingers and toes?"

Her eyebrows drew down in concentration. He could feel her wriggling her toes beneath the socks and relief flooded him. She would recover.

Knowing she was warm enough to stay alive a little longer, he crawled out of the warm sleeping bag. Against the elements, they couldn't survive through the night with just a sleeping bag.

At the sight of him her eyes widened. "You don't have any clothes on."

"Neither do you." He gritted his teeth as he picked up his wet, semifrozen clothes, waiting for a loud protest from her at his high-handed action. Not that he'd had a choice.

She snuggled deeper into the bag, not in the least embarrassed by her nudity. "Bill said to thank you for saving my life again."

"We're even. You saved me when you stopped me from going back to the plane." Still, with her talk of Bill, Sean wondered if she was worse off than he'd thought. "But Bill's dead. You were hallucinating."

"I'd rather think I wasn't. He likes the idea of us being together."

"You aren't mad that I undressed you?"

"After you took off my clothes, did you see anything you liked?" she asked with a boldness that had him wondering if the hypothermia had gotten to her after all. Or maybe he was the one hallucinating.

He struggled into his pants. "I was too busy to notice much more than the blue color of your skin."

"Liar."

She softened her accusation with a wicked laugh, her gaze focusing on one part of him that should have been shriveled from the cold but had swelled instead. Worried over her safety, he hadn't even noticed his response to her until she'd pointed it out to him.

Grateful she was back to teasing and irritating him, he zipped himself into pants that were now too tight, almost welcoming the sting of the icy cold. She didn't say another word, but as he donned the rest of his clothes, she watched his every move with a fiercely satisfied gaze, her wet, golden mane wild around her face, reminding him of a lioness.

"Where are you going?"

"We need fuel for a fire." The urge to crawl back into that sleeping bag with her made him abrupt. "Stay here."

"Like I'm going to get out of this warm sleeping bag and roam the mountain naked."

He ignored her teasing. He didn't know what to make of her new attitude. With her returning memories had come a renewed confidence in her sexuality. And his body pulsed to full alert.

"I'll be back soon."

The weather more than matched Sean's turbulent mood. Storm clouds gathered around the mountain like iron filings to a magnet. In the distance, he thought he heard the sound of a helicopter but couldn't spot it in the sky. They'd be lucky if the weather didn't sock them in with blowing snow. Buffeted by winds, hindered by his half-frozen limbs, it took longer to gather firewood than he would have liked.

He searched for pine trees that had been downed in one of last year's storms. Without an ax, he was forced to use what he could gather easily into his arms, mostly small branches for kindling. But if he wanted the fire to last through the night, he needed logs. Unfortunately, all those of good size needed splitting. He finally kicked out part of a rotten stump, hefted his find onto his shoulder and carried it to the cave. Carlie had fallen asleep again and her coloring looked good.

Too good. Her cheeks a healthy pink beneath her tan, her lips invitingly parted in sleep, and memories of her silky skin made him work all the faster. She'd been right about his lying. Even as he'd worried about her safety, he hadn't been immune to her charms. He remembered almost spanning her waist with his hands and longed to explore more of her.

His conscience pricked him. Some people when confronted by danger froze, others screamed, many

ran. To others danger could be the mother of all aph-
rodisiacs. If the adrenaline rush had turned Carlie on,
he'd be a world-class callous bastard to take advantage.

But he wanted to.

Sean made several trips before he dared stop. Even
so, he didn't think he'd gathered enough wood to last
the night. But it would have to do. Carlie needed him
to get her out of these mountains alive. Driving himself to the point of exhaustion was stupid in terms of
their future survival.

And yet he wasn't sure if he was frozen enough
to spend the night in that sleeping bag with her. And
not hate himself in the morning.

When he returned to the cave, his fingers were so
cold, he could no longer feel them. Carlie had awakened, and at the sight of him she leapt naked out of
the sleeping bag, helped him strip off his wet clothes
and tucked him in.

"I've got to build a fire," he protested.

"I'll do it."

Wearing nothing but socks, she gathered the kindling but couldn't get the wood to catch. As appealing and cute as she looked running around in nothing
but her socks, nipples hard as pebbles, he wanted her
back inside the sleeping bag where she would be
warm.

His teeth chattered. "Burn money. Wallet."

"Won't it be wet?"

"W-waterproof."

She dug into his pants, pulled out a one dollar bill
and lit it. Crunching a second bill into a ball, she lit

it using the first and then shoved the burning ball of paper into the stack of kindling.

"It worked."

"Good. Come back here."

She shook her head. "Give me a minute."

After selecting several of the larger branches, she drew them near the fire. Voracious flames reflected off her skin, giving her a tawny glow that made his groin fill with a heaviness he couldn't deny. Carefully, she spread their clothes over the branches so they'd dry, teasing him with her every graceful movement. Then she added more kindling to the fire and finally several of the heavier branches.

With the fire burning cheerily but still giving off little heat, she gathered up the pot from the survival bag, filled it with snow and left it wedged between some wood over the fire.

"Come," he insisted, patting the spot beside him. Weariness made keeping his eyes open almost impossible, yet his sex had a mind of its own, surging, ready. He intended to ignore the part of himself he had no control over. He would gather her into his arms and sleep. But not until she was back beside him.

Instead of coming to him, she scooped up some of the food supplies and tea bags. With the melted snow that was now boiling she made them tea. After handing him a steaming cup, she finally slid beside him.

Propped on an elbow, he sipped the hot tea, welcoming the heat that burned a blazing path down his gullet. She snuggled next to him, cuddly as a kitten.

Subtly, he changed position, trying to gain some distance between their bodies. She followed him like water sliding past the banks of a river, naturally and completely unstoppable.

He'd been willing to play the gentleman. But not anymore. She wasn't a virgin. She was old enough to know her own mind. He told the last remnants of his conscience to take a hike.

"I could get used to this," he teased, his voice low, watching for any sign that he might be reading her incorrectly.

"What?"

"Having a naked lady serve me hot tea in bed."

Her lips twitched in amusement. "If you play your cards right, I might serve you more than tea."

He stared into her green eyes filled with promise, admiring her bold confidence. He so badly wanted what she recklessly offered him that he'd become sensitized to her smallest movement. The silky caress of her hip against his stomach. The soft, smooth velvet of her calves entwined between his. The lush mouth he ached to taste again.

He'd been over his head with her from the moment they met. And now the subtle changes in her since she'd regained her memories had him volunteering to drown in those huge green eyes. But she was acting differently enough to make him wonder if she had an ulterior motive. They hadn't had a chance to talk since she'd regained her memories.

There was a core of honesty in her that shone through everything she said and did. She didn't have to tell him she hadn't killed Jackson—he knew it already, deep in his blood.

He shifted, pulling her on top of his chest. She straddled him, completely open to his touch. Her gold hair trailed over her bare breasts, her proud visage, reminding him of a Viking Valkyrie.

His voice was low, husky with need he could no longer deny. "Comfy?"

"Not yet." She skimmed her nails lightly over his chest, leaving no doubt what she wanted and setting his body on red alert.

He gave her one last chance to change her mind. "I don't have protection."

She grinned and wriggled her hips. "I noticed. Something's sticking into me."

"It will be if you don't—"

She lowered her mouth to his. "I'll still respect you in the morning."

He surrendered, letting her take him where he so desperately wanted to go. She wasn't the least bit tentative or patient, kissing him with the hungry ferocity of a woman who knows exactly what she likes and exactly how to take her pleasure.

He wanted to make this good for her, to nibble, to tease, to seduce. But she was having none of waiting. With one taste of his mouth, her hips plunged downward, sheathing him fully inside her sweet hotness.

"Now, that's comfy." She grinned like a cat lapping frothy cream.

She felt like liquid gold. Precious. And hotter than a firecracker on the Fourth of July.

Holding her hips still, she plucked at his nipples, causing an erotic, intoxicating sensation. Two could play this game. He began by skimming his fingers over her midriff. Her incredible eyes locked with his. Desire raced through him and it took all of his control to hold still.

He cupped her breasts, rubbing his thumb over her responsive peaks. She eyed his lips in speculation, then leaned down and swirled her tongue inside his mouth. He stroked her back and her hips bucked with a sensual promise that made thinking almost impossible.

Recognizing the pleasure she gave him wasn't just lust but from deeper emotions, he laced his fingers through her hair, kissing her with abandon. "Slow down, sweetheart."

"I don't think so." Her hips took him higher than he'd ever been.

Sweat broke out on his brow. He tried to hold back, balanced on a razor-sharp edge between flawless pleasure and exquisite pain. As she continued to move over him, currents of desire flowed back and forth between them. Her flowery scent coiled around him like a wisp of air.

She flexed a muscle inside her, firing his need with ripples of pleasure, forcing him to speak through clenched teeth. "Too fast...for you."

"Not fast enough." She pumped her hips, meeting his hunger with a hunger of her own. Riding him relentlessly, giving no quarter.

"You don't understand."

She threw back her head, arching her breasts into his hands. "What's not to understand?"

On the verge of finding out just how much control he had left, she tipped her hips, taking him deeper.

He groaned. "I'm on the edge."

"And you're going over."

Not yet. He reached between her legs, finding her

slick, hot, swelling beneath his touch. "I'm taking you with me."

He kept her locked with him, using his hands, his mouth, matching her rhythm stroke for stroke, kiss for kiss, breath for breath, until desire roared over him like a hot, breaking wave.

SNUGGLED UP IN the sleeping bag next to Sean, Carlie was as toasty as if she were lying on a heating pad. She awakened, her legs intertwined with his, feeling content and sated.

She brushed a lock of hair from her eyes and realized that sometime during the night after the third time they'd made love, Sean had replaced the socks on her hands. His stamina had been incredible, but his tenderness stole her heart.

He'd explored every inch of her; even better, she'd finally run her hands through his thick hair, traced the sharp planes of his cheeks, memorized the sculpted muscles of his chest. Making love in a snow cave with only a fire and Sean's fiery heat to warm her had been incredibly erotic.

And if last night was to be her last, she'd spent her time well. She tilted her head up to find Sean already awake, his hot look searing her with renewed heat. Even slightly disheveled, he was one of those lucky men who looked sexy with one-day stubble on his chin.

His dark eyes turned smoky and he kissed her lightly on the mouth. "Good morning."

"'Good' could get better." She wound her arms around his neck, drawing him closer.

He chuckled. "Insatiable wench."

She adored his wood-smoke scent, his aggressive mouth and gentle hands. After kissing her thoroughly, he pulled back and swatted her bottom. In retaliation she nipped his shoulder.

"Time to get up."

She eyed him with a smile. "You already are."

Exiting the sleeping bag and reaching for his clothes, he spoke, white puffs of air accompanying each word. Despite the chill in the air, his voice was low, husky and all male. "We have work to do."

"Why work when we can play?" Without his heat to warm her, the sleeping bag rapidly cooled. She rolled on her side and watched him add the last of their wood to the fire, not in the least upset by his rejection, especially when he so obviously wanted her.

He handed her her gun. "I'm not sure it'll fire after the soaking it took. Try not to rely on it, okay?"

"Sure."

He lifted her clothes off the branches and tossed them to her. "Collecting firewood is your first task of the day. Think you can handle it?"

"Are you trying to get me angry enough so I won't notice how cold these clothes are?" she grumbled.

"Got me figured out already?"

She slipped on her shirt and pants, hoping they were dry but unable to tell since the fabric was so stiff. "Why do we need a fire? Aren't we leaving?"

"Not today."

She cocked her head, thinking hard, trying to get past the sensual haze he'd wrapped her in since they'd first made love. "There isn't going to be a rescue mission. No one knows we're missing."

"That's true."

He didn't look the least perturbed by their situation, and while she loved him for putting on a brave front, their situation was hopeless. Stranded in a frozen wasteland, miles and miles from civilization, they had maybe one day's supply of food. And no way to communicate with the outside world.

Either they would freeze to death or starve. "Come on, Sean. We aren't getting out of here alive."

At her words, Sean stiffened, turning on his bad ankle with a noticeable limp. "Is that why you made love with me last night? You thought we would die today?"

"Oh, for heaven's sake." Now was no time for him to let his hormones and pride rule his head.

Patience, she counseled herself, unwilling to let his masculine pride goad her into saying words she would regret later. She forced her feet into boots still cold and frozen, despite their place near the fire. "After we crashed, I didn't think about us. I was so cold." And she'd had that odd vision of Bill telling her it was not yet time to join him. "You were warm. And once I felt you beside me, I didn't think about the future. I didn't think at all."

"So any warm body would have satisfied you?"

Despite her wish to remain calm and rational, that he could make such an accusation had her anger rising like a geyser. "Damn you. Don't put words in my mouth. I'm not like Sally or your mother." Fully dressed, she stepped closer and jabbed a finger into his chest. "I wanted to make love with you before my memory returned, but I needed to make sure there wasn't anything in my past that could hurt you."

"Is there?" His shoulders squared, his lips firm with determination, he challenged her.

"I don't think so. I never saw Jackson's killer," she added before he could ask. "I asked in town where I could find you. Andrew mentioned that Jackson was all excited about his latest assayer's report and had just headed up to the mine to meet with you. I left my luggage at the general store and followed Jackson to the mine."

Sean stood in silence, not prodding her, giving her time to put her thoughts in order. Although his expression didn't change, although he didn't fidget or shrug or play with the fire, she sensed his impatience to hear what had happened.

"I heard a man scream, then curse." She held out her hands to the fire, chilled as much by the conversation as by the frigid weather. "When I arrived in the cave, Jackson already had been stabbed."

"Did he say anything?"

"He couldn't speak." The memory of him clutching her, blood clogging his throat, his eyes wide with terror, would haunt her for the rest of her days. She realized now that he hadn't been afraid of death. He'd been afraid for her. He'd been trying to warn her, his last moments had been concern for her because he could see what she could not—a threat behind her. "As I leaned over him, something struck the back of my head. The next thing I remember was waking up and fighting with you."

Sean stared at her as if attempting to re-create the

scene in his mind. "Why were you coming to see me?"

Carlie ran a hand through her hair, wishing for a brush, her tangled hair as knotted as her confusion. "I didn't believe Bill's death was an accident."

"Why not?"

"I think he survived the crash, and right after someone broke his neck."

"Do you have any proof?"

"The autopsy report said the blow to his neck came from the side. But according to the skid marks from his tires, he was in a head-on collision with another car."

"You thought someone murdered Bill?"

"I suspected." She lifted her chin. "I wanted to talk to you about a case he'd been working on while he was here."

"He didn't talk much about his work."

"Before his death, Bill implied he'd wanted to return to Alaska to clear up some details of an unclosed case. At his funeral one of his co-workers let slip that Bill had heard rumors that gold stolen from Russia was laundered through your mine."

"Did Bill tell you that he won a two percent share of the stock from Tyler's dad in a poker game?"

She owned a share in the mine! Did that make her a target? Had they finally found a motive behind the murders?

"What are you saying?"

"If I'm laundering stolen gold then you're as guilty as I am."

"Look, I'm not accusing you. But too many stockholders have met untimely deaths. Bill, Jackson, Wayne.''

"Don't forget Tyler's father," Sean added.

"And now us."

"We aren't dead yet."

"What the hell is going on?"

"Maybe the miners stumbled across something they shouldn't have seen?"

"That would make sense," Carlie agreed. "Could they have uncovered the gold-laundering scheme that Bill was so interested in investigating?"

"I'm not sure," Sean said slowly. "We need more facts. Was Bill's neck injury similar to Wayne's?"

She would have thought of that connection had she not been hampered by her partial amnesia. Still, she was the cop. With her memories restored she could put the pieces together. A thrill that they might finally be closing in on a connection between the murders raised her hopes. "You may be on to something."

His lip drew into a thin line. "The stock may or may not have to do with the killings. We're looking for a man with skill in hand-to-hand combat and someone who knows enough about airplanes to make one crash."

Had her husband's killer followed her back to Alaska? "We were sabotaged?" She hadn't even considered the reason their plane had gone down. In the plane, she'd been too terrified of crashing to think why the engines had quit. Then she'd been too busy trying to stay warm. And later, too busy making love with Sean.

Sean certainly knew how to distract her, but she

couldn't work up even a shred of annoyance. He'd saved her life and then given her so much pleasure she hadn't been concentrating on her mission. Yet she didn't regret last night. And she couldn't think of anyone she'd rather be stuck with in the middle of nowhere than Sean.

"Those engines froze—the chances of mechanical failure of two engines at the same time is infinitesimal."

"But the engines were fine when we left."

"Sugar or syrup in the fuel tanks would take about twenty minutes to freeze the engines."

Their idle speculation might be right on target, but a bitter dismay dulled her excitement. They would never learn the truth. Not now. Even if they figured out who was behind Bill's, Jackson's and Wayne's murders and who had sabotaged the airplane, they could do nothing about it.

She threw up her hands in disgust. "Spending the time we have left on wild theories seems like a colossal waste of energy."

As if reading her unspoken thoughts, Sean spoke with a rough edge of conviction she'd rarely heard him use. "We aren't going to die."

Her throat tightened into an uncomfortable knot. "You don't have to lie to me."

Without food, shelter or any means of communicating with the outside world, they wouldn't last but a few days. If the killer had murdered Bill, Jackson, Wayne and maybe Tyler's father, he was about to add more victims to his list. She and Sean weren't equipped to hike up and down steep mountains in freezing weather and through waist-high snow. She doubted she could walk more than half a mile before exhaustion set in.

Maybe Sean could make it alone. "You could go for—"

"I'm not leaving you."

"You'd stand a better chance alone. I'll only slow you down."

"Leaving you is not an option. Either we go together or we don't go at all."

She sighed, knowing she was fighting his past and memories of his father leaving. His mother dying. Still, she had to try to dissuade him. "Look, if you go, you'll make better time. Leave me some matches and I'll stay by the fire and…"

"We have one sleeping bag and one pot to cook food."

"What food?" The concentrated provisions could be stretched to last for a day, maybe two.

Sean's voice softened, sending a swirl of heat straight to her heart. "But even if we had double the supplies, I couldn't leave you." She was about to protest again when he cupped her chin with a gentle palm, caught and held her eyes. "Listen to me."

"Then tell me the truth."

"*We* can walk out in a week."

"Right." She winked at him, but her heart hammered in her chest at the steely determination in his eyes. "And if we had wings we could fly."

Chapter Twelve

While Carlie gathered firewood, Sean carved walking sticks out of tree branches with his knife. After dumping her third armload of firewood at the cave's entrance, she rested, already weary. Trudging through the knee-to-waist-high snow proved as taxing as she'd suspected. Although Sean had insisted they eat a hearty breakfast from their limited supplies, already her stomach growled, hungry from her exertions.

Wiping the sweat off her brow, she wondered how her body could be so warm while she could barely feel her toes. "Is that enough wood?"

He set down his knife and tested the point of a spear with his thumb. "We'll need more wood to smoke the fish and to keep us warm another night."

"What fish?"

"The fish we're going to catch in Sunrise Lake." She eyed the spears with healthy skepticism, but he didn't seem to notice, carving out a rough notch below the spear point. "And if we're lucky, I'll catch a deer."

Deer? Images of eating Bambi made her stomach

churn. Although she wasn't a vegetarian, hunting, cleaning and cooking an animal were very different from the sanitized version of picking out her meat in a grocery store. Although she didn't say a word, Sean must have caught the look of dismay on her face.

He gently squeezed her shoulder. "We might catch enough fish that we needn't hunt any other animals."

"Thanks." Grateful he hadn't teased her over her squeamishness, she turned back for another load of wood.

"I won't let you starve, either."

At least she'd managed to conceal her growing fear of the dark. Ever since she'd been trapped under the avalanche, she'd been uneasy. The dark icy waters swirling over her head had increased the irrational fear in her mind. But she refused to give in to it.

No need to worry, Sean would build them a fire every night. She hoped they'd catch lots of fish. After she'd completed her wood-gathering chores and had a chance to warm up by the fire with a cup of tea, Sean led them back onto the lake to a hole in the ice, bringing their supply bag with them to store their catch.

On the frozen lake, the wind seemed chillier, the ice below her feet freezing through her boots and woolen socks. Keeping her feet warm was a major problem, and Sean had warned her that she should speak up before her toes and fingers turned numb.

He'd explained that hurrying unprepared through the wilderness led to hunger, weakness and overexposure to the weather, which often resulted in unnecessary death. Better to catch food, eat when hungry and rest when tired, stopping well before dark in protected areas. He figured on arriving in Kesky in a week or so, but healthy.

And while he explained, all she could think of was chocolate. Thick, rich, creamy light chocolate and caramels. With pecans or cashews. Life wasn't fair. Why couldn't she have lost her craving for chocolate instead of picking up a fear of the dark?

And why couldn't she relax? She figured Sean knew his mountain-man craft, but she had this almost irresistible urge to hurry. And out on the lake, she felt vulnerable. Exposed.

But no one watched them. The snow-capped peaks above the lake were as hospitable as Clearwater Beach during a hurricane. And just as intimidating. Not only didn't she see any sign of human life around them, she didn't see animals—not an eagle or a moose or a mosquito.

Sean seemed to sense where the ice was weak, stopping and carefully scraping away the snow and testing the thickness with a stomp of his boot.

"You ever done this before?" she asked.

"My father taught me when I was four years old." Sean rolled the spear's point between his thumb and forefinger. "I used to think ice fishing was an excuse to get cold, tired and wet, but now I'm grateful for the skill."

He had never spoken of his biological father with anything other than cold hatred. The six months it had taken his mother to die after the trapper had left his family must have been horrible for the little boy left behind. The hardships he'd endured were no doubt part of Sean's determination to live alone, and that saddened her.

He handed her a spear and lifted his brow with a boyish gleam in his eyes. "The secret is not to let your shadow fall over the water."

Carlie awkwardly hefted the pole, sure she wouldn't be fast enough or accurate enough to spear a fish even if she saw one. The icy blue water in the hole in the ice Sean had broken with the dull end of his spear didn't so much as ripple.

"Now what?"

"We call the fish over here."

"Are you going to sing to them?" Carlie teased.

Sean reached into his pocket and took out a few crumbs left over from breakfast and sprinkled them onto the surface. He tapped the ice's edge a few times with the dull end of his pole. "They sense vibrations."

Carlie shifted impatiently from foot to foot. "Suppose they aren't hungry?"

"Have a little faith, woman."

"Sean?"

"Um."

He stood so still, so focused on the water in the hole, she hated to disturb his concentration. And yet he was as relaxed as she'd ever seen him.

Slowly, she let out a breath of cold air on a puff of wind. "Did you ever see your father again?"

"Nope. Some trappers found his body in a crevasse the next spring."

Carlie reminded herself to inhale again. For a moment it had occurred to her that his father could have been alive, making trouble for Sean with some kind of twisted motive for revenge. But the man was dead.

"He knew the area like most men know their own backyards. Most likely the alcohol made him careless and he didn't watch where he placed his feet."

"So he didn't deliberately abandon your mother."

"The results were the same." Sean's voice hardened, and she knew by his tone he didn't want her to ask him any more questions.

"Sorry. I just wanted to eliminate any suspects—no matter how remote."

How could Sean remain so still? He stood as if carved out of ice. She could barely make out the white wisps of air that left his mouth when he breathed.

Unprepared for the sudden movement of his arm stabbing with the stick, she jumped. Then he drew back the spear and a fish flopped on the end.

"It's huge." The fish, two feet long and pleasingly plump, shone dully on the snow.

"It's a lake trout. Some of these grow up to forty-seven pounds."

Sean didn't take even a moment to examine his catch. He returned to the ice hole, his arm plunging again. Once more he came up with a fish.

"Come on. You try."

"I don't think—"

"This doesn't require thinking. Just aim and stab." Sean set down his spear, came up behind her, cocking her arm at the correct angle.

"Sean, I don't want to waste—"

"Shh. Suppose I had twisted my ankle so badly I

couldn't walk. You might be the only person who could find food until I healed."

She understood the sense of his argument. Right now she was dependent on his skill to survive, and if anything happened to him, she was as helpless as a baby. On the other hand, she didn't want to scare away the fish and waste their opportunity to stock up on supplies.

"Don't let your shadow fall on the ice until you make your move."

Several fish fed on the crumbs Sean had tossed into the hole. But they swam quickly away.

Disappointed, she started to edge back from the hole. Sean blocked her escape and tossed in more crumbs. "Wait until one turns sideways. That'll give you the best odds of landing one."

"Maybe I could just shoot it," she suggested, referring to the gun she still wore strapped to her ankle.

"Even if the gun fired, the fish might sink. Plus you'd ruin any chances of catching more than one fish per hour."

"At this rate, I'm not catching one fish a year."

"Patience."

"I'm a city girl. What do you expect? When I want a fish dinner, I make reservations at Shell's Restaurant."

Sean steadied his chest against her back. "Did you hit the bull's-eye the first time you shot a gun? Do you solve a case on the first clue? Do you—"

"Nag, nag, nag," she complained.

At least his teasing made the time pass a little faster. Standing on ice, waiting for a fish while she shivered and her hands cramped, was not her idea of fun. And yet if she hadn't been so worried about walking out of these mountains she would have been enjoying herself. Sean had a way about him that made her think she could do anything.

Determined to do her share, Carlie clenched her fingers tighter around the bark. A fish rose near the surface.

Sean helped her steady the spear, his strong hands over hers. "Wait. Wait."

The fish turned. "Now."

She stabbed. And missed. The fish ignored the pole, seemingly unaware of her intentions.

Sean smoothly jerked the pole up, and before disappointment could flash through her the stick plunged downward, guided by Sean's skill and steady hands.

The spear struck. She yanked upward, surprised at the weight of the fish, anxious not to lose her catch.

"Easy does it." As the fish wriggled and Sean helped her wrestle with the pole, Carlie heard the distinctive buzz of a helicopter.

Someone had to be looking for them.

She released the pole and waved her hands back and forth at the sky, signaling, shouting and running. They wouldn't have to clean and cook and eat the fish. They wouldn't have to spend the next seven days fighting the cold and walking back to Kesky. Hope lifted her heart. They would be rescued.

THE HELICOPTER FLEW by without dipping. Or circling. Or stopping. Disappointment sapped Carlie's energy, leaving her cold enough to shiver and so tired she wanted to cry. She headed back to Sean with her head down and shoulders slumped, telling herself to get a grip and not quite succeeding.

Sean took one look at her face and abandoned their catch, gathering her into his arms with a tenderness that made her throat close tightly.

"We're going to be fine," he assured her in a tone fraught with frustration at her obvious distress.

Disappointment clouded her normally optimistic nature. Worse, she spoke the fear that had haunted her ever since the plane crashed. "Maybe you can walk for hours through waist-deep snow, but I'm not up for that kind of physical exertion."

"Neither am I. But after I make us some snowshoes, we'll walk on top of the snow."

"Snowshoes?" Astonishment made her lift her eyes to him, where she saw nothing but sincerity and unwavering confidence.

"They won't be pretty, but they'll work," he promised.

"If you say so."

He kissed her forehead, her nose, and hugged her hard enough that she had trouble drawing a breath. "When are you going to trust me? I'll get you out of here."

"I wasn't doubting your ability—but mine."

"Doubts from a woman who caught her dinner on a spear?" He stepped back and stuffed their catch into the bag. Standing, he handed her one of the fishing spears. "Why don't you go back to the cave and build up the fire?"

She dreaded returning alone but knew the cold was wearing her down both emotionally and physically. If she let her condition deteriorate, she'd be more of a liability to him than she already was. "Aren't you coming with me?"

"Soon." He picked up his spear and added the last crumbs to the finishing hole. "I'd like to bag one or two more fish and then we'll have enough food to last until we reach Kesky."

Carlie used her fishing spear as a walking stick. She headed to the cave, gritting her teeth with every step. Although they'd broken a trail to the lake, some of the deep snow had caved in, forcing her to step slowly and carefully.

She built up the fire, removed her clothes and burrowed into the icy sleeping bag. More exhausted than she'd realized, she dozed, awakening to the scent of fish cooking over the fire.

Sean sat on a stump, the firelight flickering over his tanned skin, as comfortable in the cave as in his cabin's den. He'd already cleaned the fish and set them on top of branches that arched over the fire. But he focused his attention on his fingers that busily wove branches together and tied them with what looked like strips of bark.

"Can I help?" She started to slip out of the sleeping bag.

He shook his head, a lock of hair falling raggedly across his forehead. "No, thanks." His husky voice kindled a warmth deep in her heart. She loved him, loved him more today than she had yesterday. Loved him more this afternoon than she had this morning. Would love him more tomorrow than she did today. She wanted to take off his clothes, tease him into the sleeping bag until he made love to her again. But he must be exhausted.

"I'll go collect more firewood," she offered.

Again he shook his head, not meeting her eyes. "We have enough to last until morning when we'll be leaving."

While she'd slept, he'd not only cleaned the fish and cooked it, he'd gathered more firewood. Guilt and frustration that he'd done all the work while she'd slept stabbed at her. His efforts made her feel like a child that needed taking care of, and yet when he finally raised his head and looked at her with that hot, smoky stare, she felt all grown-up. And very glad she was a woman.

Although she recognized the lusty look in his eyes, she ached to hear the words. "What are you thinking?"

"I'm thinking you wouldn't be so tired today if I'd let you sleep last night."

"That's ridiculous. I wanted you, Sean. I wanted you last night. I want you now. And I'll want you tomorrow."

He carefully set aside the snowshoe he'd been working on, but she noted the slight tremble in his words. "That's good, because the thought of sharing that sleeping bag with you and not having you might do me in."

She opened the bag, held out her arms to him in open invitation. And didn't need to ask twice. She'd never seen a man remove his clothes with such enthusiasm.

Her breath caught in her throat at the sight of his magnificent physique. Mountain living had sculpted an athletic body out of his broad-shouldered frame that narrowed over rippling abs, a flat stomach and muscular thighs. Despite the long hours he'd spent working in the cold, he was more than ready for her, his sex hard, his skin hot.

"It's about time you got here," she whispered, skimming her fingers across his chest.

"I thought you'd never ask. Sitting there while you slept was sweet torture."

"You could have wakened me."

She saw doubt flicker in his smoldering gray eyes and realized he hadn't been sure he'd be welcome. While a little uncertainty might be good for his arrogant soul, she didn't want to play games.

He kissed her brow, traced a scorching trail to her neck and murmured in her ear. "You needed rest."

"I need you." Saying the words aloud, admitting her feelings, came as naturally as breathing. She'd never felt this alive, this cherished, this hunger boiling in her veins, heating her blood until her toes curled and her breath came ragged and slow.

She expected him to reek of fish but didn't care. Pleasantly surprised by the scent of wood smoke, pine and a tangy aroma she couldn't identify, she sniffed appreciatively. "How can you smell so good?"

"The right roots make an adequate soap. I saved you some." He grinned wickedly through a beard growing thick and soft. "I'll help you wash. Later."

She skimmed her hand over his newly grown whiskers, the soft ends tickling her palms.

He ran his fingertip down her neck, over her collarbone, then circled her breast. "Sorry. Without a mirror, I didn't want to risk shaving."

"Your beard is already soft." She kissed him. "It tickles my mouth."

"That's not all it can tickle." He dived under the sleeping bag.

She gasped at the feel of his hot mouth on her breast, his tongue shooting licks of fire straight to her groin. Wanting him inside her with an urgency that left her dizzy, she spread her legs and arched her back.

"You aren't ready yet," he mumbled from somewhere around her stomach.

Afraid he would smother, she began to unzip the sleeping bag, a difficult task since Sean's mouth and fingers never stopped testing, teasing, taunting. Her fingers trembled, but she finally opened the blasted sleeping bag, giving them more room.

At first, the cool air on her blazing skin felt marvelous. Where Sean's heated flesh touched her, she burned. But a few minutes later, despite the fire he'd kindled, goose bumps prickled her flesh where her naked skin was exposed to the air.

Sean noticed her discomfort immediately. "I don't want you to catch cold."

Shivering but hungry for more of his touch, she was shocked when he stood and lifted her into his arms. "What are you doing?"

"You need a bath."

Through a haze of sensual pleasure she recalled stories about Scandinavian people cutting holes in the ice and swimming in freezing water, and considered the custom barbaric. No way was she taking an ice bath. "I thought you said I needed warming up."

"That, too."

Sean walked out of the cave and around a bend in the hillside. The last heat from the fire dissipated from her skin and a frigid breeze made her teeth chatter. "Where are you taking me?"

"I explored this side of the mountain when I was searching for firewood," he answered evasively.

She looked over her shoulder at tracks that indicated he'd come this way before. Just a few footsteps from the cave and hidden by a snowdrift, steamy puffs rose into the air. "You found a hot spring?"

"Alaska boasts thousands of hot springs." Sean set her feet in the shallow end of the rock pool. "Too bad I didn't find it right after the plane crash."

Blessed heat had her hurrying to sink up to her neck beneath the pool's surface. "We could have frozen to death and been only steps away from heat."

"But we didn't." Sean reached for her and nuzzled her neck. "Now, where were we?"

Hot water against her cold skin made her bones melt with a lassitude she hadn't felt since she'd arrived in Alaska. Closing her eyes against the darkness and mountains and snow, she gave herself up to Sean's touch, reveling in the warmth of the water lapping her breasts, imagining bright yellow Florida sunshine, beaches and home.

An image of Sean suddenly superimposed itself in her thoughts. Without opening her eyes, she knew his gray eyes glittered with a smoky passion in a way that made her uncaring of her surroundings. He stroked her face, her hair, her breasts, and she clung to him, throat aching, aware that without Sean in her life, home would be an empty place.

This last year, she'd been in turn angry over Bill's

death, sad and lonely. But now she'd found a man to love and she vowed to experience every breath of his seductive attention while he focused on her.

He adored her with his hands, his mouth, entwining his legs with hers, drawing her as close as two people could possibly get. The tension he'd built in the snow cave returned with hurricane force. Floating in the water, she felt light as a rain cloud ready to burst.

Night came early and fast in the Alaskan winter. The sun had set and the moon had risen. Twinkling pinpoints of light on a black velvet sky shone down on them, a backdrop for the spectacular northern lights of the aurora borealis.

"Sean?"

"Um. Do you know you taste as sweet as chocolate?"

She reached under water, found his hips and drew him inside her. Sean gasped and held completely still. She caressed his back, urging him to move.

Urgent need rocked her. She bit his shoulder. "I...can't...wait."

"Neither can I."

He pumped his hips. She clung to his waist, matching him move for move until the calm surface of the pool rippled with whitecaps. Every muscle in her drew taut in anticipation. Blood roared in her ears. And then she exploded, raw pleasure ripping through her in mindless, sizzling bliss.

Later, much later, after her breath steadied and her heart rate settled to normal, Sean washed her tenderly. Then she steeled herself against the cold and they prepared to make a mad dash for the snow cave.

She insisted on running, claiming they would freeze if Sean carried her again. Soaking wet and naked, laughing like children, they raced to fire, food and the shelter.

Out of the darkness, a shot rang out, singing past Sean's head. A second shot whizzed by Carlie's ear.

Chapter Thirteen

"Keep running."

Sean grabbed Carlie's arm and under the bright moonlight helped her hurdle the last few snowdrifts and push on into the safety of the cave. That they were naked and exposed was his fault. Instead of dallying with her in the rock pool, he should have been concentrating on keeping her safe. But he'd let his growing feelings for Carlie sway him against his better judgment.

They pulled up short beside the fire, breathing hard. Sean tossed a T-shirt to Carlie. "Dry yourself and dress."

She did as he asked, but first she strapped her gun to her ankle. "Maybe I should fire my gun—"

"And let him pinpoint our location?"

Carlie twisted her hair behind her head and wrung out excess water. "Whoever is out there might be a lot more cautious if they think we're armed. Slowing them down gives us time to escape."

Not a bad idea. But he disagreed. "I'd rather not give the shooter a hint of our location."

"What about our fire? Won't the shooter see it?"

Sean shook his head. "Judging from the angle of those shots, we should be concealed behind the bend. For all he knows, after we raced away we kept going down the mountain."

"And?"

"We might need every bullet you have. I'd rather not waste one."

"Okay." Carlie shrugged, seemingly inclined to follow his lead. She'd been a trooper since the crash, and Sean realized how lucky he was to have her with him. Another female might be hysterical. Another woman would have spent her time complaining and blaming him for their predicament. Not Carlie. She was practical and strong, having the sense to recognize and admit what she didn't know.

He broke off a piece of fish and popped it into his mouth, the smoked trout's flavor light and sweet, reminding him of his empty stomach. "Let's eat and pack up first."

Carlie paused in her dressing, one foot inside her pants. "We have time for a meal?"

"And a nap. Not even a sniper can hit us in here. We'll eat, sleep and leave before dawn." He saw no need to mention that he intended to do a little midnight reconnoitering and discover exactly who and what they were up against. While Carlie rested, Sean could circle the area, pick up tracks and hunt the enemy.

"I don't like that look in your eyes," Carlie muttered with a shake of her head.

"What look?" Sean kept his face neutral, wondering how she could read him so easily—as if he transmitted his thoughts on a wavelength only she could pick up.

"The you-stay-here-and-I'll-go-after-the-bad-guy look."

"I'm not—"

"Oh, please." Fully dressed she faced him, her fists planted on her hips. "Don't lie to me. You're itching to go out there—" she pointed at the cave's mouth "—and track down that shooter."

"It's not a bad idea," he admitted a bit sheepishly.

"But you're forgetting something."

"What?"

She sat on a log by the fire and ran her fingers through her hair to help dry her locks. "That's exactly what the shooter will expect you to do. And meantime, you'll be leaving me alone." She raised her eyebrows as if to say *gotcha*.

"You don't play fair."

Carlie didn't look frightened or even angry, but determined. "I figure the safest place on this mountain is next to you, so I'd rather you didn't go wandering off."

She had a point. He'd figured on staying between her and the shooter, but in the dark, he couldn't guarantee that as he advanced, the attacker wouldn't circle behind him. Nor could he deny his irritation with her rationale. She *knew* he wouldn't leave her in danger and used her knowledge to get her way. Until now he hadn't realized she could manipulate him so easily, and he didn't like her using his own feelings for her against him.

And yet how could he argue with her logic? As much as he wanted to go after the shooter, leaving her unprotected wasn't a good option. He considered moving their camp to a more hidden location and discarded the idea.

Uncomfortable that she'd boxed him in so easily, he removed the fish from the branches and packed all but the one they would eat for dinner. Frozen, the cooked fish would keep for weeks. With his knife he cut the remaining fish in half and placed it in the pot—their only eating utensil.

He sat beside Carlie on the log. "Careful. It's hot."

She picked off a crisp piece, blew to cool it and offered a bite to him.

They ate, then he finished making their snowshoes and stashed the fish in a tree to avoid bears stumbling upon them and their food. They slept in their clothes, awakening before dawn. He insisted they eat again, drink the last of their tea and put out the fire.

"Ready?"

Sleepily, Carlie rubbed her eyes and looked at her feet. "I don't know about these snowshoes."

"Walk in a shuffle. By noon you'll be a pro."

After pointing Carlie in the right direction, Sean retrieved their cache of fish and slung the pack over his shoulder. With his free hand, he grabbed the fir branch he'd cut yesterday.

Following in Carlie's struggling footsteps and dragging the evergreen, Sean swished the trailing branch over their tracks, hiding their trail. With any luck, they'd walk back to Kesky without being spotted. And yet if the shooter knew they were aiming for Kesky, he could all too easily move ahead of them and waylay them in an ambush.

Planning a more circuitous route and reminding himself not to tire Carlie out, he resigned himself to a slower pace and added another two days to his original estimate of how long it would take them to walk home. He didn't let himself think that a slower pace would give them more time together because any thoughts of her leaving caused him pain. Instead he concentrated on his mountain lore.

Slow and easy is best in the woods. He heard his father's words in his mind. Would a day or two matter? The important thing was to stay warm, fed and dry. And of course, to avoid whoever wanted them dead.

They plodded through the day, keeping to the cover of pine trees and shadows, Sean concealing their tracks as best he could while Carlie cursed her snowshoes. If only she'd try to walk with them and shuffle. That night, at the first site he checked, a large cave on the side of the mountain, he found a bear had already claimed the spot for its winter hibernation.

It took him an additional hour to find another cave. One look at Carlie's pinched lips, and he knew she'd forced herself to go on for longer than she should have. The woman never complained. He made her rest while he cached the fish, started a fire and cooked their supper. She fell asleep as soon as she slipped inside the sleeping bag and he held her close.

He would make sure she rested more often. He'd hidden their trail thoroughly enough that even the best tracker shouldn't have been able to follow them. And they'd gained enough distance from this morning's campsite to ease up on their pace tomorrow.

While Carlie slept, Sean circled their camp to get a lay of the land. Although he felt confident they had eluded the shooter, he still wanted an escape route—just in case. Ever mindful of Carlie's vulnerability as she slept, he didn't go far. A glance at the stars assured him they'd maintained their southwesterly direction and he carefully noted landmarks that would keep them on course through another day.

Sean scanned the mountain, memorizing the notch he intended to keep on his right shoulder, and spied a sparkle of something that didn't belong. Glass? Metal? Something manmade glinted, maybe a reflection caused by a fire hidden from view.

Damn.

Either their pursuer had picked up their trail or guessed their route. Stealthily keeping to the shadows, Sean retraced his path back to Carlie. As much as he would have enjoyed discussing their options with her, he didn't consider waking her. She needed rest—especially if they had another hard day of hiking ahead.

Annoyed the shooter had been able to follow them, Sean slammed his fist into his palm. He'd covered their tracks, kept to the woods. How had the man tracked them? In his mind, he retraced their path. They'd walked over a rocky area for an hour and changed directions before putting on the snowshoes. And they'd crossed a frozen lake where they'd left no tracks at all. Their pursuer would have had to be psychic to follow their trail—because they hadn't left one.

Okay. So why was their pursuer close by and still out there, waiting to take another shot at them? Jackson had taught Sean that after he'd eliminated the obvious, he had to look at the options remaining, however improbable they might be.

Sean ducked inside the cave and searched their meager supplies. It took him an hour to find the metallic bug in the bottom of Carlie's backpack.

No wonder their pursuer had no trouble finding them! With an automatic homing device, the shooter didn't need to follow a trail in the snow.

His first instinct was to smash the little electronic device. But then Sean picked up his knife with a grin. He'd spied some willow bark close by and he could strip the tree and make a snare. Trapping a rabbit, attaching the bug to the animal and then setting it loose would keep the shooter off their trail for hours. And tomorrow, he and Carlie could set a leisurely pace in another direction. By the time their pursuer discovered his ruse, they would be long gone.

THREE DAYS AGO Carlie had stopped swearing at her snowshoes. Two days ago she'd stopped walking with her head down to prevent herself from tripping. And yesterday, she'd let herself appreciate the spectacular beauty of these snow-capped mountains. While she never wanted to call Alaska home, thanks to Sean, the wilderness no longer frightened her.

After that first day, Sean had kept the pace reasonable. Gradually, during the short days, she'd slipped into a rhythm—plant walking stick, shuffle, shuffle. And at night, she and Sean had discovered their own rhythm of loving under the stars.

He told her stories from his boyhood, opening himself to her in ways she hadn't imagined. And yet they never spoke about the future. Alaska was his home, where he ran a business and roamed the mountains freely. And she didn't want to stay. She missed her family, her job, her friends. She missed boat rides on Tampa Bay, soaking up the sun on the beach.

Even if she could overcome her reluctance to give up her Florida home, she had no future to offer a man. Although her memory had returned, she still had no idea who had killed the old prospector. She hadn't forgotten her prints on the murder weapon, Jackson's blood on her sleeve. Without solving the murder, she would stand trial and most likely be convicted.

While walking, she racked her mind for answers. Suspicions swirled in her head, but she had not one iota of proof to offer concerning her own innocence. Just because Sean believed she was innocent was no reason to think twelve strangers on a jury would do the same.

Sean stopped walking and pointed down the mountain ridge. "Looks like we've got company."

A half mile downhill, a group of people clustered around the clearing in front of the Dog Mush Mine. They were too far away to make out individual features, but Carlie thought she'd spotted Tyler's neon ski suit in the group.

As they hiked down the mountain, Carlie frowned at the men gathered around a campfire. "I thought the mine was closed."

"It is."

A half hour later they'd trekked to the mine and joined Tyler, Roger, Andrew, Marvin and Sally grouped around a fire at the threshold of the Dog

Mush Mine. The group rushed toward them, frowning, smiling and asking questions.

"See," Tyler shouted with a grin. "I told you a search party wasn't necessary."

Marvin clapped Sean on the back. "I figured you'd show up soon."

"Yeah, what took you so long?" Roger muttered.

"We heard your plane never made it to Fairbanks." Sally stood as tall as any of the men, except Sean. "We were fixing to rescue you."

Carlie tried not to look suspiciously at any of them. Which one of these people had sabotaged their airplane? Who had stalked them through the mountains? Wearily, she removed her snowshoes. "How long have you all been here?"

"Just since this morning," Tyler told her, fingering a gold earring. "We weren't sure the plane had gone down until the phone lines came back up."

Could Tyler have arrived in Kesky ahead of them and picked up that news in town?

Sally thrust a cup of coffee into Carlie's hands. "Are you hungry?"

Carlie nodded, surprised to see the woman on the mountain. "But no fish."

The group settled around the fire. Sally dished Carlie and Sean up some franks and beans. Carlie ate while Sean told his friends and business partners an abbreviated version of their story.

"The plane engine was sabotaged?" asked Tyler.

"Yep." Sean put down his coffee cup. "We think that whoever killed Jackson may also have killed Carlie's husband, Bill, as well as Wayne Riker."

Carlie would never forget the odd angle of the

miner's neck. Intuition told her the same man that killed Wayne had murdered her husband, but she needed proof.

"But Riker died in an avalanche," Tyler argued.

"Maybe. Maybe not." Carlie sipped her coffee, watching their faces for clues. Sally looked puzzled. Tyler unhappy. As usual, Carlie couldn't read Marvin's eyes. Roger hid his expression behind his thick beard.

Andrew, the kindly manager from the general store, frowned. "What makes you think there's a connection?"

"We aren't sure," Sean told them, failing to mention that everyone who had died owned stock in the Dog Mush. But except for Jackson's shares that were now Ian's, none of the shares were that valuable, certainly not enough to kill for. "Bill died in Florida in a car wreck. His neck was broken."

"Just like Wayne's," Carlie added.

Tyler flinched, his face going white. Carlie recalled how he'd been on the mountain on the day of the avalanche. He'd also been around when the wire had been strung between two trees. And again after Wayne's death. But proximity didn't mean he'd committed murder.

Sally glanced nervously at Roger. "Weren't you and Andrew in Florida last year?"

Roger threaded his fingers through his beard. "No law against fishing."

Marvin's gold tooth flashed. "I was in Maine when Bill died." He turned to Tyler. "Weren't you at some water skiing event in Tampa?"

"I was invited." Tyler's voice rose with indignation. "They wanted to see what a snow skier could do on water."

Across the fire, Carlie and Sean exchanged a long look. Three of the men had been in Florida at the time of Bill's death. Although their questions weren't narrowing down the suspects quickly enough, the killer didn't know that. Perhaps they could shake the killer up into making a mistake.

"Any of you all have experience in hand-to-hand combat?" Carlie asked.

Sally chuckled. "I've decked a man a time or two."

Carlie would bet she had. "How about military experience?"

Roger slapped his knee with disgust. "I was a Green Beret and Andrew boxed his way through the navy. And I've seen Marvin pull some fancy moves around the card table."

Sally sighed, resting her elbows on her knees and planting her chin in one palm. "Tyler, didn't your daddy teach you some kung fu?"

"I also wind sail, skateboard and sky dive," Tyler boasted with a sly look.

Sean folded his arms across his chest. "Why don't you all tell me where you were two days ago."

"I don't have to answer you," Roger muttered. "But I will. I was up in the mountains. Hunting."

"Alone?" Carlie asked.

He patted the rifle beside him. "Just me and my gun."

"I was skiing," Tyler said.

"Anyone see you?" Sean asked.

Tyler hesitated. "Probably not."

"And Marvin was with me most of the day," Sally added.

Charlie thought hard. Tyler and Roger didn't have alibis and Sally and Marvin had only each other to verify their whereabouts.

Roger turned and stared at Carlie. "What about you, missy? Has your memory returned?"

"Yes." An idea began to form in Carlie's mind. A dangerous plan. Sean caught her eye and shook his head slightly, as if aware of what she might try and warning against it. But Carlie wanted to flush out the killer. They'd tried to narrow down the suspects through logic, and it hadn't worked. And right about now she was willing to take a big risk. Well aware of Sean's disapproval, she ignored him and the sudden excitement racing through her. She had to make a stab at drawing out the killer or face the likelihood of spending the rest of her life behind bars.

"You know who killed Jackson?" Sally asked.

Everyone turned to Carlie. The group seemed to collectively hold its breath.

Carlie fidgeted, then forced her hands to still. "My memory has returned. But if I come right out and accuse the guilty party, it's my word against his."

Sally's eyes shone bright and curious. "So tell us, anyway. Who killed Jackson?"

"Luckily," Carlie continued, ignoring Sally's question, "now I have the proof I need."

"What kind of proof?" Roger asked, impatience coloring his tone.

"A motive." She kept her voice confident, hoping Sean wouldn't give her game away, hoping the sharp-eyed gambler wouldn't read the lie in her eyes.

"You see, *I* had no reason to kill Jackson, but now I know why the killer did."

"Why?" Sally asked, her voice choked. "Jackson never did anyone any harm."

Carlie pulled her biggest bluff. "Jackson was killed out of greed."

"Greed?" Tyler scoffed. "That's ridiculous. I think you're making up a story to save yourself."

"A good cop never tells everything she knows." Carlie spoke calmly, implying she knew much more.

The airplane crash had jarred her memory back, but she still couldn't name the killer because she'd never seen him. There was nothing for her to remember—but the killer didn't know that.

If she pretended that she knew who the killer was, he would have to come after her—reveal himself. And perhaps if she was lucky, very lucky, she could turn the tables.

If not, she'd rather go down fighting than spend the rest of her life in jail. Hoping Sean would forgive her, she tried to appear confident.

Roger swore under his breath. "Who killed my brother?"

Marivn chewed his toothpick, his upper lip curved into a small smile. Andrew threw up his arms and shook his head in frustration.

And Sean silently seethed. He didn't move. He didn't tense. He didn't say a word, but the gray in his eyes smoldered with a fury she hadn't seen before. Carlie refused to look at him again. No matter how angry Sean became that she'd risked her safety, the decision was hers. Her future was at stake. She'd risk herself as bait to clear her name.

Carlie stood and stretched. "I'm telling the rest of what I've figured out to the authorities. They can handle the case from there. How soon will someone fly in?"

Sean stood and took her elbow, his voice low and all the more deadly for its whispery softness. "We need to talk." Without giving her much choice, he practically dragged her into the mine and out of the hearing of the others.

He pulled her along so quickly, she didn't see much more than a blur of rock walls supported by timbers. The dirt floor descended gradually as the odor of old dust and stale air filled her nostrils.

Sean finally halted but kept a firm grip on her arm. "Are you crazy?"

She shook her arm, attempting to free herself of his touch, but he refused to let go. "I've lost a husband. I've been accused of murder. I've been shot at. Your plane was sabotaged and I'm tired of running." She swallowed hard, knowing she verged on tears. "I've spent the last five days eating nothing but fish. And I'm not running anymore. I don't have to—"

"I'll help you—"

"How touching," Tyler said, sneering behind them. No longer in his neon ski outfit, he'd changed into a miner's hat, dark jacket and work pants.

Carlie focused on his hand and saw Tyler aiming a gun at them. He fingered the trigger. "Get your hands up. Both of you."

"Tyler, you won't get away with shooting us," Carlie said, trying to think, her thoughts scattered with fear. While she'd kept Tyler on her mental list of suspects, she had never really thought he was the killer. His boyish charm had fooled her. But despite her earlier words, she still didn't understand his motive.

Tyler motioned with the gun, backing them farther into the mine. "Move. And don't think of calling for help or I'll shoot whoever comes in here."

Sean spoke firmly as if to a two-year-old. "You can't kill everyone."

"I don't have to," Tyler mumbled. He stayed four feet behind them, giving Sean no chance to attack, giving Carlie no opportunity to reach for the gun always strapped to her ankle.

Tyler forced them deeper into the mine, past the spot where she'd awakened next to Jackson's bloody body.

"The others will be suspicious," Sean told Tyler, his tone calm and deliberate.

"Keep going," Tyler ordered.

They walked deeper into the mine. Cold seeped down her collar and up from the frozen rock beneath her boots. Blackness enveloped them like a coffin. And while she could barely make out the hefty beams that supported the walls and roof, the passageway continued to narrow.

Even as she feared the darkness, she sought a way to use it to her advantage. She considered faking a fall and scrambling for her gun and nixed the idea. Tyler followed too close behind her. If the rock walls became constricted enough to walk single file, Carlie might be able to dive for her gun without Tyler's noticing.

"You killed my husband for stock in the mine," Carlie said, trying to distract Tyler, putting the pieces together now that he'd revealed himself. Normally, stock couldn't be stolen, it had to be legally transferred. But if Tyler had forged Bill's signature on stock in a privately held company, then sold the certificate, he could pocket the money and be long gone before anyone caught him. "You killed Wayne and you killed Jackson. Did you steal Jackson's stock certificates, too, only to learn that Ian held the bank note? That must have made you angry. All that killing and so little to show for it."

Tyler sneered again. "You don't know anything."

Sean slowed his steps and turned toward Tyler, placing his body halfway between Carlie and the gun. "Maybe we can make a deal."

"No deals."

The kid was hard as nails. Why hadn't she been able to see the warped mind behind that little-boy smile? Even now he didn't seem the least bit nervous, but cocky and confident. He must have been terrified she would openly accuse him, secretly pleased when she hadn't.

Her plan had worked too well. If she died in this attempt, she would be sorry to miss what the future might have held, but she didn't regret her actions. And yet she'd never meant to jeopardize Sean, and fear for him almost paralyzed her. He didn't deserve to die, and her reckless plan had trapped him into sharing her fate. While she'd envisioned having to say goodbye to him, she hadn't thought it would be this permanent.

She kept waiting for the mine's passageway to become narrow enough to go for her gun. Sean casually dropped between Tyler and her.

Soon, she promised herself. Wait a little longer.

Only, waiting might not be an option. She forced herself to ignore the darkening passageway. Drawing air into her lungs made them ache. "How do you work down here? I can't breathe."

"The air circulation fans are off," Sean told her. "If we go much—"

"Shut up," Tyler ordered. "Sounds echo down here."

Behind her, Sean spun, the air from his sudden movement whipping up dust. Carlie dropped to the dirt and jackknifed for her gun.

Snatching up her pants leg, she jerked her weapon from the holster. Behind her, a shot was fired. A bullet hissed through the air and thunked into the ceiling.

Carlie heard the sounds of flesh striking flesh. Behind her the men fought in a life-and-death struggle. Someone cursed.

"Sean?" She couldn't see past the clouds of dirt in the darkness, choked on the dust.

Frantically she crawled toward the last spot she'd seen Sean, staying low to avoid bullets. Reaching out, she felt the hard leather of a boot. "Sean, is this you?"

She couldn't risk shooting the wrong man.

In the darkness, the two men rolled. She couldn't tell Tyler from Sean.

While the men struggled over the weapon, fear gripped her. Wanting to help, unable to shoot for fear of hitting Sean made her stomach go cold with dread. She'd never forgive herself if she shot Sean.

A string of bullets whizzed into the ceiling. The

loud crack of splitting timber was her only warning of something gone terribly wrong.

Rocks pelted down at her and she raised her arm to protect her face. Out of the darkness a body came flying and knocked her flat, forcing the wind from her lungs.

"Don't move," Sean whispered in her ear, his voice her only grip on sanity in a world that had gone mad.

She struggled to breathe, telling herself at least he was alive. And all the while, rocks, dirt and timbers collapsed around her, burying her. Burying him.

Chapter Fourteen

Sean had thrown himself over Carlie the moment he'd realized the ceiling support had been knocked out, causing the cave-in. His lunge to protect her had been more instinctive than a thought-out plan. Once the ceiling rained dirt, rocks and timber upon them, he could do no more than hold Carlie and shield her.

Grimly, he suspected his meager efforts to save her wouldn't be enough. This offshoot corridor of the Dog Mush was old and not as solid as their current operations. Just from the sound of the debris falling, Sean knew that digging themselves out could take hours. The stale air would give out long before then.

Choking on the dust, he smoothed back Carlie's hair. "Are you all right?"

"Can you roll off of me?" she asked in a tight voice.

He did as she asked, unable to see his hand in front of his face in the complete darkness. "Where are you hurt?"

"My leg is trapped. But there isn't any pain."

Sean skimmed his hands down the length of her. Her leg was encased in a mound of dirt, rock and timber. Gently, he started to dig her out, but the wall shifted. Pebbles rolled down.

"Sean, stop. The wall is unstable. If you keep going it may trap you, too."

Sean sank back on his heels in frustration. Her lying there trapped while the air diminished in the tunnel had him almost frantic with worry. No one knew where they were, and even if they came looking, the miners might not even realize this cave-in was new. They could walk right past the tunnel's entrance and never realize Sean and Carlie were trapped behind the debris.

"What happened to Tyler?" Carlie asked.

In his concern over Carlie's predicament, Sean had forgotten about the traitor. "This may sound callous, but I don't ca—"

"He was wearing a miner's hard hat. There was a light on it."

Maybe with a light, he could see well enough to dig her out without causing another cave-in. At least one of them was thinking clearly. Sean crawled along the debris-strewn floor, bumping into Tyler's body. He checked for a pulse and found none. "He's dead."

"There went my defense," Carlie muttered, though how she could think about her case at a time like this he didn't know. The kid's hard hat had fallen to the floor and Sean claimed it, turning on the light and placing the hat on his head to leave his hands free.

He turned toward Carlie, shining the light on her trapped leg.

"Sean! Look." She pointed to the wall above her.

Fifteen feet high and twenty feet long, a spectacular gold vein gleamed thick and bright under his light. "The mother lode."

"Do you think Jackson knew the gold was here?" Carlie asked.

"The assayer's report probably indicated he was digging toward the vein and—" Hardened mud plopped off the wall. "Stay there a second."

"I'm not going anywhere." She turned her head, following him with her eyes.

"Someone found this vein and hid the gold with mud."

"Tyler?" she asked.

"But why would he keep it a secret?"

"Maybe he intended to steal from you," Carlie suggested.

"Maybe." But gold was heavy. And it would be hard to conceal a secret mining operation beneath Sean's nose. But they could work out Tyler's nefarious scheme later. First they had to get out of here.

Sean returned to Carlie and shone his light on the wall of debris trapping her. If he could move a massive support timber aside, he figured she could slide out. "I need a lever."

"A what?"

"A pry bar. Something to wedge beneath that timber so you can wriggle free."

Sean searched the rocks and mud, ignoring the gold glitter on the wall. Right now he'd trade the entire mother lode for Carlie's freedom.

"What's down this tunnel? Does it lead anywhere?"

That was his woman, always thinking. "I'm not

sure. Jackson worked these old tunnels years and years ago. It could end within fifty feet or go on for miles.''

''Well, then you better get going.''

''What?''

''You can't free me. You can't help me by staying and holding my hand.''

''I'm not leaving you.''

''Then we'll both die.'' She shooed him on with a wave of her hand. ''Go do your mountain-man thing. Find your pry bar and come back and rescue me, tough guy.''

He understood the logic of her reasoning, but every cell in his body told him to stay. If he left her, she could die. Alone. Without him to protect her she'd be helpless.

No, she wouldn't.

Carlie was the strongest woman he'd ever known. She was resourceful. She wouldn't fall apart. And he loved her. Loved her with a force that gave him the strength to leave her. While he was gone, he wouldn't be a bit surprised if she managed to dig her own way out.

''What are you waiting for? Our air's running out.'' Carlie laced her fingers together and pillowed her head. ''You'll need the light. I'll just take a little nap.''

Sean knelt beside her and planted a kiss on her mouth. Yearnings to stay almost weakened his resolve and reluctantly he pulled away. ''I won't be long.''

''Take as long as you need to. There's nothing you

can do for me here." She bit her bottom lip and he could see she was holding back a question.

"What?"

"Are there rats in here?"

He shook his head and lied. "They've found a much warmer place to spend the winter." But he gathered a pile of fist-sized rocks and placed them within easy reach of her hands. His throat closed at the effort she made to be brave, to make it easier for him to leave her. "Just in case—"

IN THE DARKNESS, Carlie had no way of judging time. She'd lain still, watching the last of Sean's light disappear, holding back her tears, fearing she would never see him again. Now she was alone in the dark with a corpse. At least she'd managed to conceal the pain in her leg from Sean because she'd suspected he never would have left if she'd admitted she was hurting.

Sitting up, she dug away a handful of soil. But she had no better luck of rescuing herself than Sean had. Dirt and rocks tumbled down, and restlessly she lay back again, knowing she would have to wait for Sean's help.

Concentrating on relaxing, she tried to conserve her air, tried to forget her fear of the darkness. She let her mind drift to images of Sean. Recalled his making love to her. Recalled his wood-smoke scent, his smooth voice, his eyes smoldering with passion. Even now she might be carrying their child.

Her arm curled protectively over her womb. If it was possible, Sean would return for her. If anyone could rescue her, he would find a way.

She heard him returning long before she saw the light. "Sean?" She called out weakly, the air unfit to breathe.

"Don't talk," he ordered, and she wondered if she were hallucinating.

But then he touched her, the scent of him enveloping her like a heady perfume. "Found a shovel to pry the timber."

He shoved the end deep beneath the timber, put his shoulder under the handle. "On three. One. Two. Three."

Sean grunted, prying the timber away from her, shifting its massive weight. Red-hot pain shot through her leg. Ignoring her injury, gritting her teeth against the agony, Carlie dragged herself free.

"Go. Crawl. If this wall comes down, I don't want you under it."

Not trusting her injured leg to take her weight, Carlie rolled to her belly, crawled on her elbows and dragged her legs. The shovel handle cracked, the sound echoing like a gunshot. The wall rumbled. Rocks slid.

But she and Sean were free. Free to suffocate.

Every breath seemed useless, doing nothing to ease her aching lungs. Sean slung her into his arms and she didn't remember much of their nightmarish journey, eventually noticing that the deep blackness had turned to gray. Slowly the air turned crisp and clean. By the time Sean set her down in a part of the mine she'd never seen before, she'd lost enough blood to make her woozy and weak.

She saw a camp stove, food, a chair and several blankets on a cot.

"Where are we?" she asked weakly.

Sean placed her on the cot and frowned at her bloody leg. "Jackson's last camp, I think." He left her for a moment and returned with a bottle of whiskey and strips of cotton to bind her leg.

With his knife, he cut open her snowsuit and then her jeans. She sat up to look at the damage and he pushed her back down. "Don't look."

"It's that bad?"

He uncapped the bottle of half-full whiskey, tipped it to his mouth and swallowed. Then he held the bottle over her wound. "This is going to hurt."

"Ow. Ow. Ow-ow. Owww!"

"That was the worst. Now just let me bind it up. I suspect you need stitches but your leg doesn't look broken."

Her stomach turned queasy.

Carlie shut her eyes tight, not opening them until Sean finished with his makeshift bandages. He leaned over her, his face filthy from dirt and dust and perspiration, his eyes full of concern, and she thought he'd never looked more handsome.

She had a sour taste in her mouth and longed for a drink but shuddered at the thought of liquor. "Is there any water?"

Sean walked to the mouth of the tunnel and returned with an icicle. While she sucked on the treat, the cold liquid revived her and she looked around. Apparently Jackson had used this site as his last before nearing the rich vein of ore. A stack of foodstuffs caught her eye, in particular a bright gold tin of chocolates.

"Sean…" She pointed to the chocolates and her

stomach groaned in anticipation. "Would you bring me that tin?"

He walked over to the food and surveyed their choices. "Soup would be better—"

"I've a hankering for chocolate." Her mouth watered. Maybe it was her weakened condition, but she was craving something sweet.

Sean lifted the tin, hefted it and brought it to her. "Don't get your hopes up. It may be empty."

While she held the can, he pried off the lid. "Nothing but old receipts."

She gave him the can, disappointed out of all proportion. She was close to the edge, her nerves more ragged than she'd realized.

Sean started to set aside the tin, then grabbed a piece of paper from inside. He waved the paper slips in the air, his baritone edged with excitement. "These are receipts from the bank to Jackson—I recognize the account number."

Her mind was fuzzy. "What are you saying?"

"Jackson paid off my college loans."

She lifted her chin. "That means that Ian Finley lied to you."

"He must have been working with Tyler."

Suddenly the pieces of the mystery clicked into place. "Tyler found the gold vein and hid it until Ian could get his hands on Jackson's stock."

"Only a forty-five-percent share isn't enough for majority control of the company. So Tyler killed your husband and Wayne Riker and stole their stock certificates for their two-percent shares. I wonder who was next on his list?"

With Jackson's receipts, Carlie could clear her

name of murder. Bill would get the justice he deserved. Although Tyler had already paid for his crime, Ian Finley would not go unpunished for killing her husband or Wayne Riker. Once again she was a woman with a future, and despite the pain in her leg, she felt as if a weight had been lifted from her shoulders.

At the sound of voices outside the cave, Sean protectively placed his body between Carlie and the others. Within moments Sally, Roger and Andrew crowded around her with another man she identified by his uniform.

The law had arrived.

SEAN HELPED CARLIE hop off Doc's table after having twenty stitches to close the gash along her shin. While local anesthesia had dulled the pain in her leg, nothing would dull the sharp pain in her heart. Haskell, with Ian Finley in handcuffs, had offered Carlie a ride on his plane back to Fairbanks. From there she'd catch a flight to L.A., then on to Houston before landing at Tampa and joining her anxiously waiting family. So saying goodbye to Sean had come much sooner than she'd expected.

Now all she had to do was say goodbye to Sean.

Words wouldn't come. Despite the tightness in her chest, she would make it through the next few minutes without crying. Sean put his arm around her waist and she leaned into him for support.

"Just a few more steps. I've a snowmobile waiting outside to take us down to the river."

She'd never been so grateful for the noisy roar of the machine. When they arrived at the river, Sean took her by surprise, swinging her into his arms. "I don't want you to trip and open those stitches."

Placing her hands around his neck, she pressed her cheek against his chest, breathing in his scent, wishing he'd at least asked her to stay. But he hadn't. He hadn't shared his thoughts, his feelings, his plans, and his silence hurt more than she wanted to admit to herself.

He nodded to Haskell, ignored Ian and carried her up the steps and settled her into her seat. When he slid in beside her, she assumed this was goodbye.

But Sean methodically strapped himself in.

"You're going with me?"

He raised one dark eyebrow. "You think I'd let you go alone?"

Why shouldn't she fly alone? With Ian in custody and Tyler dead the chances of someone sabotaging this plane were minuscule. "You're going with me to Fairbanks?"

"Yes."

Her heart skidded and skipped a beat. "You sure?"

Sean grinned down at her. "Maybe I haven't made myself clear."

"You certainly haven't."

"Then I'll rectify the situation." His gray eyes smoldered with a heat that set her stomach fluttering. Gently, he cupped her chin and raised her gaze to his until she could see the black circles around his gray irises. She'd never noticed that about his eyes before and wondered what else she didn't know about him.

"I love you."

Confusion settled over her like a heavy coat. Had she heard him right?

"What did you say?"

"Pay attention, woman. I said that I love you."

"You love me?"

"That's right."

"I love you, too." Her words popped out before she had time to think about them.

He didn't move, didn't even appear to breathe. They locked gazes and she felt as though her every defense had just been bulldozed by an avalanche.

He'd picked one hell of a time to announce his feelings. Why had he waited this long to tell her? Did he expect her to stay in Alaska with him? She had to think, but her thoughts kept careening sideways.

He'd said he loved her.

His thumb ran along her jaw, tempting her to kiss him. "And I want us to be together."

She couldn't make her thoughts line up in order. Her heart beat wildly in her chest. "I suppose I could stay another week."

He shook his head. "Not long enough."

How could she make up her mind so quickly about whether or not she could live the rest of her life in a town one quarter the size of her high school? Could she stand to live without daylight through most of the winter? Could she manage to keep her sanity through month after month of snow?

If staying meant sharing a cabin with Sean, she believed she could be happy. But what of her job? Her family? She would miss her friends, too. And yet she couldn't say no to this man. She supposed she would live on the moon or Antarctica to be with him.

"Haskell!" She tapped the lawman on the shoulder. "Stop the plane. I'm staying."

Sean exchanged a look with the lawman and rolled his eyes at the ceiling. "We're both going to Florida."

Carlie's jaw dropped. She knew she must look stupid, but Sean's statement had left her flabbergasted. "You're coming with me? But what about the mine?"

"We'll come back in the summers to reopen it."

Warmth and happiness flooded her. She didn't know whether or not she was pregnant, but she would like to have Sean's child. Instinctively she knew he'd be a wonderful father. "But your business? What about all that gold—"

"It's been there for thousands of years. It'll keep until summer. But you—" he tapped a finger on her nose "—you need me to keep you out of trouble."

"I do?" She chuckled happily. "I mean...I do."

HARLEQUIN®

INTRIGUE®

43 Light St.

Outside, it looks like a
charming old building
near the Baltimore
waterfront, but inside
lurks danger...
and romance.

"First lady of suspense"
Ruth Glick writing as
Rebecca York returns with

#558 NEVER TOO LATE
March 2000

Scott O'Donnell had believed he'd been betrayed
by Mariana Reyes, yet he still was unable to resist
the attraction that had consumed him six years
ago. Their reunion was laced with secrets and
danger. With a killer on their trail, Scott had to
protect Mariana—and the daughter he never
knew he had.

Available at your favorite retail outlet.

HARLEQUIN®
Makes any time special ™

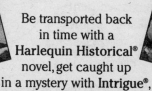

Coming in January 2000
Classics for two of your favorite series.

SECRET VOWS by REBECCA YORK & KELSEY ROBERTS

From the best of Rebecca York's

43 Light St.

Till Death Us Do Part

Marissa Devereaux discovered that paradise wasn't all it was cracked up to be when she was abducted by extremists on the Caribbean island of Costa Verde.... But things only got worse when Jed Prentiss showed up, claiming to be her fiancé.

From the best of Kelsey Roberts's

THE ROSE TATTOO

Unlawfully Wedded

J.D. was used to getting what he wanted from people, and he swore he'd use that skill to hunt down Tory's father's killer. But J.D. wanted much more than gratitude from his sassy blond bride—and he wasn't going to clue her in. She'd find out soon enough...if she survived to hear about it.

Available January 2000 at your favorite retail outlet.

HARLEQUIN®
Makes any time special ™

Amnesia...an unknown danger...
a burning desire.

With

HARLEQUIN®

I N T R I G U E®

you're just

A MEMORY AWAY...

from passion, danger...and love!

**Look for all the books in this
exciting miniseries:**

**A NIGHT WITHOUT END (#552)
by Susan Kearney**
On sale January 2000

**FORGOTTEN LULLABY (#556)
by Rita Herron**
On sale February 2000

**HERS TO REMEMBER (#560)
by Karen Lawton Barrett**
On sale March 2000

A MEMORY AWAY...where remembering
the truth becomes a matter of life,
death...and love!

HARLEQUIN®
Makes any time special ™